PTERANODON CANYON

TIM MEYER

EVIL EPOCH
PRESS

Published by Evil Epoch Press

Edited by Jenny Adams

Cover Design by Chad Lutzke

ALSO BY TIM MEYER:

Novels:

In the House of Mirrors

The Thin Veil

Less Than Human

Sharkwater Beach

Primal Terra

Lords of the Deep (with Patrick Lacey)

The Switch House

Kill Hill Carnage

Limbs

Dead Daughters

Malignant Summer

Paradise Club

Wormwood (with Chad Lutzke)

Collections:

Worlds Between My Teeth

Black Star Constellations

Demon Blood Series:

Enlightenment

Gateways

Defiance

PTERANODON CANYON

THE BEAKS * ANOTHER DRINK FOR CHARLIE * THE MAN WITH NO LIPS * FINN WAKES UP * OLIVER SMITH COMES TO TOWN * TWO BEASTS AND A WHOLE LOTTA BULLETS

Gleaming metal slips between the Pterosaur's beak and crest, biting into the feathery surface and the forgiving bone of its skull. Red wells, drowning the clean silver. The saw's teeth rip into the marrow, making noises that would curdle the blood of any ordinary man. But the six degenerates holding down the massive wings don't flinch, don't move, don't even blink as the cut-man works the tool back and forth, elegant movements that require impressive force, mobility the muscly-armed brute has and executes effectively. The magnificent creature screams, a weak cry for help, a plea for its circling brethren to descend from the bright skies and provide rescue. But no such rescue comes, for the beasts of these precious canyons have learned: sail too low, dine on bullets; sail too high, the sun'll bake ya.

The fallen Pterosaur, *awash in the dying day's purple shadows, has more holes in its wings than insect-eaten jungle leaves. The canyon sand is soaked with dark blood. There's one last feeble attempt to escape, one hopeful flutter of its massive wings, but the men are weights that can't be lifted, and the graceful creature is granted one more breath, one more squawk, one last look at the tan-shaded world it occupied, those cloudless blue heavens it once called home. The animal draws its final breath, ceases all movement, and stares off into a world far beyond this one.*

The kneeling men ease up but only so much, as if, even in death, the beast poses some invisible threat.

"Are ya done?" asks one of them, as he lifts a hand from the wing and scratches the scar under his right eye. "My belly's a rumblin' something fierce." Arching his back, he scans the deep magenta above. "Bet them birds just as hungry."

Tanner, the cut-man, glares at him, discontinuing his effort, letting the saw blade stick deep within the creature's ivory extension.

The speaker shrinks back, and then avoids that glaring eye, that sole orb—the other hidden behind a black patch. The story of that eye's disappearance is somewhat of a mystery among the men, but with the aggressive nature he demonstrated on the Pterosaur's beak, one might have thought the flying dinosaur had something to do with it. "Sorry, Tanner. Didn't mean nothin' by it. Just speakin' my thoughts is all."

"I'm done when I'm done, boy," Tanner growls. "Not a second sooner."

His pause doesn't last long, hardly a breath, and he's back on the job a second later, ripping and sawing, gaining depth in the bone now, ignoring the spurting blood that practically covers every square inch of him, his clothes, those tremendous puddles that soak the sand beneath his sinking boots.

The beak begins to flex much like a timber when the saw is almost through. He thinks he can break it off, sacrifice a clean cut if need be, but the bird's dead, done floundering, and his friends in the sky don't seem to mind very much at all. In fact, Tanner gets the sense they're more like vultures, not hunters, considering how they circle, waiting for expired flesh and muscle to become unoccupied, ready to swoop down after the killers have left, before decomposition runs its course.

One final hack and the bird's beak is released. From the open cavity, blood pours out like a spill of tea, and dangling gristle soaked in red follows closely behind, clinging to the cranium's inner hollow.

Takes three men to carry the long beak back to the wagon.

Next, Tanner starts on the wings, hacking and slashing, blood arcing with each heavy stroke. Doesn't take long to pare through the thin bones and cartilage. Quarter of the time it took with the beak. Ain't much money in wings, but the men like the way they taste, and they'll make for a good snack come later.

After he's done, the men finish loading the wagons, stocking them full of the severed parts, beaks, wings, and meat alike. All six of them, each led by a sturdy, reliable horse.

Tanner wipes sweat from his brow as the sun begins to sink on the horizon, washing the canyons in this beautiful-yet-smoky pale purple shroud.

Shortly after, the wagons take off, leaving behind dozens of bird carcasses, the clay earth stained from the evil that white men do.

IN THE TALL shadows of the long afternoon, Oat Creek sat near the Arizona/New Mexico border, a cozy spot where some would argue that one side of town was Arizonian, and the other side was New Mexican. If you planted your feet right, you could be in both territories at once. But silly arguments like that were never solved in Oat Creek, and they were rarely passionately argued for, and even rarer than that did they ever end in a thirty-pace-turn-around-and-shoot showdown. Unlike places such as Deadwood, Dodge City, and Tombstone; the stories that came from those towns were enough to turn away your average feller. But Oat Creek—now that was a good place. Some would lobby it was the premiere spot to raise a family this far out west, in case you wanted to leave the east coast and explore the opportunities the west offered. Even though the gold rush had ended about twenty years prior, there were still people digging, plenty of jobs to go around for any working man. Construction too. Yep, Oat Creek had plenty of jobs, and criminal activity, violence of any kind, came in small doses.

It was why Charlie Archer had moved out here in the first place. Charlie was tired of those *other* places, tired of going in for a drink at his favorite saloon and coming out with a black eye or, sometimes worse, bruises on his knuckles from giving some other asshole a black eye. Bruised knuckles messed with his memoirs, the collection of notes he was keeping on his life, the adventures he'd had since moving out here from Kansas about six years ago.

Memoirs. *Shit*. He sure didn't enjoy writing them, but they kept the demons away.

" 'Nother drink, Charlie," asked Avery Wolcott, already pouring the brandy, anticipating the answer. Charlie wondered what would happen to that drink if he turned it down. Go to waste, he reckoned, and who was Charlie Archer to waste anything, let alone a beverage that helped take away the nightly pains, both of the internal and external sort.

"Sure thing, Ave," he said, looking over his shoulder at the saloon doors, biting his lip, waiting for those springy hinges to give way any moment now. "Appreciate you."

"You look nervous tonight," Avery said with a low chuckle. "Haven't had a *T. rex* roll these parts in almost six years, so no need to eye the door like it's got teeth."

"Can't help it. Man from Washington is coming to meet me, and I haven't the foggiest what it's about."

"Washington?" Avery wiped down the bar top with a dirty rag that probably put down more uncleanliness than it picked up. "Pinkertons after you or something? Shit. Washington, huh?"

"Haven't done a thing. Pay the tax man like everyone else. Can't imagine what the government would want with little ol' Charlie Archer."

"Maybe they want to give you some work?"

Charlie had considered that the likeliest of scenarios. Having been one of the more successful bounty hunters out in these parts, he'd earned himself quite the reputation. Just last year he had brought in two wanted men—Derek Markel and Lance O'Grady—all by himself, two men considered to be extremely dangerous in the eyes of the law. But Charlie had tracked them down and roped them up, done all of it while they were alive, and turned them into the authorities. Paid quite a few bucks, enough so he didn't have to work for a while. His last attempt to bring in another one of the country's most wanted went a little south—Brock Roth was eaten by a pack of *Deinonychus* near the Texas border. All Charlie had left to turn in was some bones the little pack hunters didn't like. Luckily for Charlie, the bird-like beasts didn't gobble up the man's wedding ring, and Brock's widow had been able to confirm that it was his. Didn't pay much that one, but considering Charlie had almost suffered the same fate, barely got out of there alive, well—*successful* was merely walking away with all his limbs attached. The couple bits he had earned on that one was nothing but a nice bonus.

"Man say when he was coming?" Avery asked.

"Didn't. Sometime after sundown."

"Well," the bartender said with a radiant smile, "looks like you got time for another drink then."

"Haven't even started in on this one."

"Well, shit then—drink up, boy. You need to relax is all."

Charlie did need to relax. But something about the man's letter, recalling the desperation in those words, had him unable to sit still.

Whatever the man was going to tell him, Charlie was very interested.

ELINOR WATTS STROLLED DOWN the main drag, trying to keep her balance. She laughed at something she thought was funny, but immediately forgot what that was—this had been a good night, a very drunk night, and Elinor tended to enjoy drunk nights the best. She passed a few horses tied to their hitching posts, three to be exact, and then, from the corner of her eyes, spotted a pack of *Compy-who-zee-what's* (she never did remember the little bastards' names) eyeing up the buffet of fresh meat left right out there in the open with no place to escape to, should there be an attack. She stopped, turned to the small green lizards hunched on two feet, looking like skinny chickens with no feathers. They were timid creatures, hardly brave enough to execute a full-on assault with this much activity around. Not like a *T. rex* would, should one or two stroll through here, and nowhere near as determined as pack-hunting predators like the *Velociraptors* she had once run into out in the Utah territories nearly a decade ago. No, these were nothing like that, and, if she were to run over to them with her hands up, making threatening noises with that boisterous voice box of hers, they'd scatter like shattered glass.

But she didn't do that. It was late. She was drunk, lazy and tired, and the *Compys* were a good fifty feet yonder and hardly worth the effort it would take to stumble over there. Instead, she tipped her hat to them, almost as if wishing them a spell of good luck going forward. Then, she bounded off down the street, in search of her destination, a place called The Oyster, a name, which she had to admit, being on the Arizona/New Mexico border, didn't seem to fit the location very well. The Oyster painted a different picture in her mind, one of some cozy seaside town somewhere up on the New England coast, fishermen boats and steam ferries, smoke rising up off the water of some cold, gray morning, some eldritch sea monster paddling gently below the still, steel blue. Not sand and dirt and canyons and so much sun. However...The Oyster was where she was headed.

Because she had a date.

Not a traditional date, but a date, nonetheless. A man from Washington who had written her by letter. Okay, so it wasn't a date at all—more like a meeting—but a girl could dream, couldn't she?

"Hey there, cute thang," said a voice from a shadow she had already passed.

Part of her knew no good would come from stopping and

turning and engaging, but sometimes she couldn't help herself; in fact, she rarely could.

"Well, hey there yourself, stranger," she said, flashing the shadow an interested smile. She placed her hands on her hips and pouted her lips. "You gonna come out from them shadows and give a lady a proper 'hello?'"

Slowly, the man did move from the shadows, extricating himself from the thrift shop's clapboard exterior. When he stepped into the moonlight, she saw his face, and she knew her own face did a thing, a thing she wasn't particularly proud of. She'd seen ugly men before—men whose faces were born ugly, an unfortunate result of bad genetics or some complicated birth. Men who'd suffered burns or animal attacks. But this—this was different, and oh-so hard to look at.

"Does my appearance disturb you?" he said in a way that couldn't rightly be categorized as *offended*. More flattered. It eased her mind and simultaneously put her on guard.

"No," she said, "just wasn't expecting it, that's all."

The man smiled. "What were you expecting?"

This question and the way he asked it sobered her some. "Don't know really."

"Raptor attack," he told her, touching the mask of scars, the lumpy, shiny skin that had repaired itself so repulsively. The man had no lips, just a hole where his mouth was. The skin around them sagged where it should be tight, and there were so many lines and craters in his face that it was hard to gain a sense of what he might have looked like prior to the unfortunate event that had left him ugly. "Was lucky to live through it."

"I'm sorry."

"Why? You didn't do this," he said, referencing his own misfortunes once again with a wave of his hand, like a nomadic magician might over a crystal ball. "Or this." He lifted his untucked shirt and revealed two long pink lines, giant keloid scars that streaked the length of his belly. "Those dewclaws are a real bastard now. Don't remember most of it—passed out at some point—but I'm told all my intestines were on the outside of me, that my crew had to stuff 'em all back in, like when you pack a suitcase for a long trip but only want to bring one piece of luggage."

"That's...I'm so sorry."

"Like I said. You didn't do it. What you sorry for, girl?"

"Well...it was nice meeting you. I must be going now. I'm late for an important date." She flashed him a courteous smile, bent her knee some, and then turned toward The Oyster. The saloon was still a good distance away, and if this man decided he wanted to attack her, she thought she could outrun him even in this drunken state.

"Shit," he said, "I know who you are. Damn, knew you looked familiar. You're Elinor Watts, ain't cha?"

At this, she stopped. Spun toward him, her thumb resting on her Winchester. "Who are you?" she asked, dropping the warmth from her voice.

"Just a lonely guy looking for some company." He flashed a smile, a mouth full of wooden teeth. She suspected the raptors had taken them too. "Say, you want to skip that date and party with me instead?" He showed her the unlabeled bottle he'd been sipping from. It was almost empty, nothing but a few swigs left. Clear stuff. Probably 'shine. Or, at this point, 'shine mixed with mostly backwash. "Know a place down the road where we can get nice and cozy."

"How do you know who I am?"

"Shit, everybody knows Elinor Watts. Famous gunslinger. Heard you once won a shootout tournament, defeated Wild Bill himself. Ain't that right?"

"You know the West and its stories."

"Calling bullshit on it, then?"

"Call bullshit on a lot of things, partner."

"Well, shit." He spat a lengthy stream through the hole she considered his mouth. "I can take a hint. Just wanted to introduce myself, that's all. You have yourself a fine date, miss."

She didn't say goodbye. Instead, she turned and fast-walked toward The Oyster, unable to help the feeling that she was being followed. Stalked. Not just by the odd man with no lips—but also by the eternal darkness this world provided.

FINN HAMPTON JUMPED out of a dream. In it, he'd been making sweet love to two beautiful women with enormous breasts, but about halfway through the women turned into bloodthirsty dinosaurs, bearing the heads of some apex predators with dangerously sharp teeth and a heated passion for human meat. They tore him apart, butchered him savagely, and then he woke up screaming, his throat stripped raw, feeling like someone had poured some acid down his gullet.

"What is it?" asked the woman next to him as she caressed his back with long (so long they were beginning to curl at the ends) fingernails. He wished he'd remember their names once in a while, especially in times like this. A name can come in handy. Made him look like less of an asshole when he remembered. Made their interactions, their indecent bedroom tangos, more personable and less of a transaction. Men who went to bed with women without knowledge of their names were widely considered brutes, especially in Oat Creek, good of a town as any. And he wasn't a brute. Quite the opposite, in fact, or at least —that was how he saw himself.

"Had a bad dream," Finn told her. "But I'm okay now."

"Aw," the woman said. *Woman.* More like a girl. He hoped she was of age to participate in the lewd acts they'd performed on each other earlier. He hadn't been that drunk, though. Sober enough to have noticed a thing like that. "Well, lie back down and I'll give you something to forget all about it."

"Yeah?"

"Yeah," she said, pushing him back down until his head hit the pillow. "Relax some."

He placed his hands behind his head and closed his eyes as the woman kissed his chest, his belly, and then the happy spot below his untamed pubic hair.

"Oh," he said, enjoying the moment.

And then he heard a hard, wet crunch. A violent sound, one that brought with it a swell of pain. His eyes shot open and he looked down, his worst nightmare now a reality. The head of a *Tyrannosaur* rested between his legs, biting down on his crotch, its dagger-like teeth puncturing his flesh, blood welling up all around him, staining the sheets with angry strokes of red. The incredible pain pulsed through him, every muscle throbbing, every nerve feeling like a drop of hot wax.

He sat up and screamed, loud as he could.

Darkness.

But no pain.

And no *Tyrannosaur.*

Just Finn Hampton and the dark, empty room. The vacant space on the bed next to him. No one there at all.

A knock on the door.

"Mr. Hampton? Mr. Hampton? Was that you?" The voice was

Shirley's, the woman who occupied the apartment next to his. She and her two kids had lived there as long as he had, maybe longer. She had lost her husband in a stampede about two years prior. "Herd of *Triceratops* got him" was the story she'd told. He'd been hunting *Parasaurolophus* out near Utah and got caught up in it. Something about the story never made much sense to Finn, knowing what he knew about *Parasaurolophus* and their migration patterns. They always headed south for winter, and Shirley claimed her man had died in late December around Christmastime. Finn had always suspected the story was a cover—that maybe Mr. Shirley had been caught in Utah with his pants down with some floozy and Mrs. Shirley found out about the whole ordeal. Had him killed, or worse—did the killing herself, and maybe fed his remains to a pack of super predators.

"I'm here, Shirley. That was me."

"Well, you dying in there or what?"

"Nope, not dying. I mean—maybe. We all dying, ain't we? Some of us slower than others, yeah?"

"Mr. Finn, it's much too late for philosophical musings." She *tsk*ed him through the door. "And Philip and Marshall have to get up for school tomorrow. So can you keep your weird sex dreams to a minimum?"

Yes, he had told her about the strange dreams. But in his defense, he'd been really wasted that night, hadn't remembered speaking a word of it come the next morning. Since then, she occasionally questioned him about it. Bringing it up during times like this, which he guessed was appropriate given the late-night screaming fits.

"I'll try to control myself, ma'am. I appreciate you keeping tabs on me."

"Okay then."

"Well, good night now."

"Good night, Mr. Hampton."

Finn lay with his head on the pillow. He couldn't really guarantee he wouldn't slip back into one of those dreams. And the only thing Finn really liked to do when he couldn't sleep was drink and fuck—and there was only one place he could do the both of them. That was down at The Oyster.

He swung his feet off the bed and began to search for his pants, unable to remember exactly where he'd put 'em.

"ARE YOU CHARLIE ARCHER?" asked the man who dressed like he *was* from Washington. He was wearing a silver-gray vest over a white shirt, a ruby-red tie, and black shoes that were so shined that Charlie thought he might go blind if he stared at them long enough.

"Yes, that's me." Charlie stood to shake the man's hand. "Oliver Smith?

"That is what my parents named me."

"Pleasure. Hope you had a good trip? Washington is quite the ride."

"It was pleasant, yes. Used the railroad mostly. First class, of course."

"Of course."

Oliver glanced around the room, as if Charlie wasn't the only person he was scheduled to visit tonight.

"I'm sorry, are we expecting someone else?" Charlie saw no

one noteworthy in the crowd of loud drunks and working women looking to make an easy buck, nor the few sleeping drunks in the booths in the corners.

"Yes," Oliver said, almost disappointed that the third member of their party wasn't already there and waiting. "She might be running a few behind." He pumped his hand, beckoning Charlie to take back his seat. "Guess we'll get started without her."

"I'm here," said the woman pushing her way through the saloon doors. The tails on her long duster flapped with the gust of wind that followed. A few of the patrons glanced up at the new arrival, but their eyes didn't linger much—they went back to their drunken conversations, uproarious laughter and lewd remarks spoken absentmindedly, behavior that was never shunned in a place like The Oyster.

Charlie offered the woman his hand. She hesitated to return the gesture, but when they locked eyes, she finally met him halfway. He bent his knee out of respect for the lady—something his wife would have appreciated, had she been here to witness the introduction.

"Charlie," he said, nodding.

"I know who you are," the lady said, not sounding enthused by their interaction. "Bounty hunter. Brought in Markel and O'Grady just a few months back, no? And alive? Impressive," she added before throwing the bartender the signal, code for get me a shot of whatever, dealer's choice. "How'd you manage that?"

"And you are...?" Charlie asked, his curiosity raging.

"This is Elinor Watts," Oliver answered for her.

"Elinor Watts. Ah, the famous gunslinger."

She batted her lashes and looked the other way. "Please."

"I'm serious," Charlie said, straightening his posture in front of such a celebrity, not wanting to appear the least bit weak. "You're a big deal 'round these parts. You know, people talk about you like you're a phantom. Some ghost that haunts the West."

"Well, *boo,*" she said, jokingly, or so he thought.

"You joke, but it's true. You're a living legend, and I...I have to admit—I was starting to believe you weren't real."

"Well, here I am. In the flesh."

"All right, you two," Oliver interrupted, having a seat, asking them both to do the same by tapping on the table.

Elinor grabbed her shot the second the bartender put it down in front of her, kicked it back, and took her seat across from Charlie. "Might as well get down to business."

"Business?" Charlie asked. "That what this is all about?"

"What else would it be about?" she asked him. "Man from Washington travels all the way out here—what the hell else he want to discuss besides business. Ain't that right, Mr. Smith?"

"My friends call me Smitty. You may too, if it does ya fine."

Charlie turned for the bar and grabbed the three beers the bartender provided. Setting them down on the table, Charlie finally found his seat, not planning to move from it once the conversation began.

"No thank you, Mr. Archer," Smitty said. "Haven't had a drink going on ten years now."

"Well, good for you," Charlie told him, and then offered the extra to Elinor, who only looked at the first beer with some caution. "Not poisoned, Mrs. Watts."

"Call me, Nellie." She took the beer, and a sip. "My friends call me Nellie."

"Nellie it is, ma'am."

"And never ma'am."

"Well," Smitty said, interrupting yet another exchange, "now that you two are well acquainted, let's talk business."

"Please do," Nellie added.

"So, you're both wondering why I traveled so far out here to talk when a simple letter stating my offer would do. Fact is, this is a big job, and...it is of the secretive sort. Meaning, we couldn't risk a message getting intercepted by nefarious factions."

"Figured that's what you meant when you said 'secretive.'"

"Indeed, Miss Watts. Indeed." Smitty licked his fingers and then dipped his hand into his briefcase, the leather so fresh that Charlie could smell it over the beers and harsh body odors that permeated the place. "What I have here is an exclusive contract."

Smitty laid the contracts down on the table, one for each of them. He sat back in his chair, folded his big arms across his chest, and then bore a proud smile.

"Is that number right?" Charlie asked, bypassing the details and getting to the figures—truly the only thing that mattered. He'd hunt *rexes* up along the coast of California for the right digits. Long as it paid well, hell, he might even hunt packs of raptors by his lonesome. "Can't be right."

"Number's right," Smitty confirmed.

Nellie held the sheet close to her eyes. "President Grant signed this?"

"Signed by Ulysses S. Grant himself, that's true."

"Well, shit." Nellie put down the contract, revealing the big smile that had been behind it. "Count me in."

"Wait," Charlie said, and even though he'd had a few rounds prior to the conversation, he definitely wasn't intoxicated enough to legally bind himself to some half-brained agreement. "There's...there's little to no information on the job itself."

"Well, that's where the secrecy comes in," Smitty said. "Can't have the details on the contract the same way I couldn't mention them in the letters. But I'll give you the rundown. And I think you'll both be very interested in them, perhaps for different reasons. But interested all the same."

"Well, please," Charlie said, resting back in his chair. "I'd love to hear them."

"I know you would." A smile and a wink, and Smitty was shifting in his seat, taking a raconteur's perch on the edge of his chair. "Tell me, what does the name Francis Burner mean to you?"

AT THE VERY mention of Burner's name, Charlie saw red. Felt like someone had reached into his chest, removed his heart, and spiked the beating thing on the floor in front of him. Then stepped on it afterward, grinding his vital muscle with aggressive toes. Charlie almost leapt out of his seat so he could choke Oliver "Smitty" Smith, for no other reason than he had brought the savage's name back to his memory.

Not that he'd ever forgotten Francis Burner. Not that he ever could. But it was buried there in the back of his mind, where most dead things were. Certainly not all dead things, because some dead things had the power to come back. In dreams, in thoughts. The dead came back all the time, but Charlie Archer had done a pretty good job of keeping them at bay.

"I know he's dead," Charlie said.

"Is he?"

"Aye. He is."

"Well," Smitty said, a knowing smile spilling across his face, "I am here to inform you that Francis Burner is very much alive."

That familiar swell of hatred caused an invisible flame to heat his face.

"Hold your horses, Mr. Archer, before you go and react in a manner that you may regret sometime later."

"It's impossible. Train derailed six years ago—I watched it with my own eyes." If he closed his eyes and concentrated hard enough, he could still see those awful fires burning, but he didn't dare to. "No survivors."

"I regret to inform you that, despite how it may have appeared to you at the time, Francis Burner survived that catastrophic event, and he's alive and well, and up to his old tricks again."

Charlie didn't want to argue too much considering the offer in front of him, though, hunting ghosts wasn't exactly his specialty. "Say it's true: what the hell does Francis Burner have to do with a thing like this?"

"Well, I'll tell you—plainly, this contract is for the capture of one, Francis Burner, along with all of his known associates. All of them wanted, as you can imagine, dead or alive. But we want them recognizable, intact, so if they get eaten by a couple of roaming *Tyrannosaurs*, swallowed up full, you get none of the aforementioned purse. Is that understood?"

Charlie didn't know how to react, so he just nodded along and sipped his beer, suddenly wishing he was drunker.

"Francis Burner is a menace," Nellie said, finally breaking her silence. "If he is still alive, what does President Grant want with him?"

"On the surface? Well, Francis's activities haven't been exactly legal over the years—before or after his supposed death —something you both know and know pretty damn well, so there's the whole not paying taxes on income angle. Plus, there are the illegal activities themselves, which pose both national and local threats. Train robberies—"

(a fiery blaze, towers of black smoke, the charred remains of the passengers scattered across the rolling green hills, dead eyes that see no more)

"—and then, of course, the murders he's responsible for, the ones we goddamn know about, at least. But...recently, our boy Frankie and his crew of sock puppets have gotten themselves into a bit of poaching trouble, and they've been hitting some protected lands out in Wyoming, getting into *Pteranodon* poaching."

"*Pteranodon* poaching?" Nellie asked. "That illegal now?"

A faint grin appeared on Smitty's face. "Well, why yes, it is. The Pteranodon Preserve Act of 1872 was signed into effect just two years ago, despite a lot of people's whining, mostly game hunters and those who made a killing off the poached beaks. But the fact is, these creatures are on the verge of extinction and there has been a lot of talk in Washington about a colossal effect certain species could have on the environment, should they drop off the face of the planet."

"Never heard of such a thing," Charlie said, still unable to unpack how Burner fitted into all of this. Just thinking about the possibilities was enough to send him into an uncontrollable rage. Sensing his blood bubbling, he pushed the past from his mind, burying it deep like he had his wife's corpse all those years ago, their child next to her. "Sounds almost silly."

"Well, can't say I agree much either. But some uppity scientists from New York City, the real know-it-all types, are predicting some great ecological disaster, should these animals go the way of the Dodo."

Nellie almost choked on her beer. "Dodo? The fuck is that?"

"Sea bird. Gone. Erased from history. Too many of them were killed for their meat and beaks. Some of these assholes in New York are claiming the harsher winters in years past are the result of their untimely demise, but, come on—common sense doesn't back that theory, and I'm not much for conspiracies. But..." he said, seeming tired of this longwinded explanation, "...Ulysses signed the act two years ago, only so he could cut a deal with Congress and pass a separate piece of legislature. All in all, it worked out because now he has even more of a reason to go after Burner, making him the most wanted man in America. Trouble is...no one can locate him. He operates under the radar, using this man..." Again, he dipped into the briefcase, and when his hand returned from the well of knowledge hidden deep in the expensive leather, he threw down the photograph. It was of a man Charlie didn't recognize but judging from his bulky neck and crazy-eyed stare—well, only one eye, the other was sporting a black eyepatch—he was one mean son of a bitch, that was for sure. "Name's Billy Tanner, and he's about the craziest fucker you'll ever set eyes on. Heard a rumor he once ripped out a man's eyes and ate 'em up like grapes right in front of his wife and kids. No rumor on how he lost his own eye, though. Whatever the cause, Tanner keeps that one to himself. Man asked him once, but the tale speaks of Tanner skewering his gonads with a steak knife, so...no one's asked since."

"Sounds like just the vermin Burner likes to associate himself with," Charlie added, and no one disagreed. "Where can we find him?"

"Well, Wyoming is where he was last spotted. Tanner that is. Locals spotted him near Cheyanne Falls, not far from a spot known as *Pteranodon* Canyon. The now *protected* lands which our boy Burner and his crew is poaching, making himself a goddamn killing on 'dactyl beaks." He tapped the photograph of Tanner. "You find Tanner, you make him squeal like a slaughterhouse hog, and he'll give up the secret whereabouts of our old pal Francis."

"If he's alive, that is," Charlie couldn't help but add.

Smitty's tired eyes grew a tad bit heavier. "He is. I promise he is."

"And..." Nellie asked from behind her beer. "...if this Tanner feller doesn't squeal?"

"Well, that's why the contract says dead or alive, young miss."

Charlie watched her face react to being called "young miss", and although he knew she hated it, the numbers on the agreement were enough to keep her quiet.

"All these years, I thought Burner was dead," Charlie said in disbelief. An incredulous laugh escaped him. "Well, damn, mister—you just about spun my world upside down."

"Apologies in that regard," Smitty said. "Know it's mighty sad to hear that news, being what he did to your family and all."

"What'd he do to your family?" Nellie asked.

Charlie didn't answer. He couldn't remember a time anybody was so bold to ask that question, and hearing it now, he couldn't find the proper way to answer it. Replying with, *Well, he killed them is all,* seemed somewhat disrespectful to their memory. But speaking about the whole ordeal and how it had come to be seemed almost a bigger disgrace.

So he didn't say anything.

"I'm sure the two of you will happen to discuss it on your ride out to Wyoming. You leave tomorrow, if you want to go ahead and put your Hancock on them-there papers." He offered them pens after dipping their tips in the little container of ink.

Nellie didn't hesitate. She grabbed the pen and scribbled her name on the allotted space. It took Charlie four times as long just to think about it. But he didn't need to. Once he had seen the numbers and heard that Francis Burner was still alive, still alive even though he'd watched him die almost seven years earlier, his body gone in a roiling fireball of death—well, once he had heard that he could kill Burner all over again, he knew he'd sign.

And so he did.

"Well, I thank the two of you for doing business with the United States Government. May God bless."

Charlie, hardly a man of God, only nodded. Nellie smiled.

"Before I go," Smitty said, standing up from his seat, "I was told to give y'all this." He reached into the briefcase and withdrew two dirty-yellow stacks of bills. "Per diem."

"Well, shit the shorts," Nellie said, running her finger along the edge of the brick, not counting it, but simply admiring the generous gift.

"I can't think of anything else to say other than good luck to you both, and please reach me by telegraph if you need anything else." He tipped his hat. "And, if you need anything before tomorrow morning at nine, I'll be at the Red Lion down on South Street."

Smitty headed for the door.

Charlie and Nellie only stared at each other.

Seconds later, the whole world began to shake.

FINN WAS GETTING his pants on when the first sound of thunder shook the world. He had one leg through, the other one halfway down as the lantern on the dresser vibrated. Stopping what he was doing and glancing out the window, he felt a spike of dread run through him, a cold chill coiling around his bones. A woman screamed from somewhere down the hall, another one of his neighbors. Not Shirley.

Wrestling with his pants, he was finally able to get them on. Finn tossed on the first shirt he saw, and then grabbed his effects, his belt and the harness holding his two most precious possessions—his two Colts, single action army revolvers, the ones that never left his sights for very long. The only time he didn't keep eyes on them was when he was sleeping (when they remained tucked under his pillow) or when he was making love (when they also remained tucked under his pillow). In either case, they weren't too far away, certainly not out of reach.

And that was because Finn constantly feared times like this. Feared those massive beasts with the long teeth.

"Shirley?" he asked, stepping out into the hall. Some of the other neighbors had already wandered out, inquiring about each other's experience with the strange thunder. "Shirley, you and the kids all right?"

Shirley opened the door a crack, her blue eyes and auburn hair making a late-night appearance. "Fine, yes."

"Good. Listen to me. Gather them up real close now. Get into a closet. Maybe hide under the bed. And don't come out until the thunder stops. You hear?"

Shirley nodded, the slow, reluctant kind.

"Good girl."

"What are you going to do?" Shirley asked, the second he made for the end of the hall, the stairs.

"Going to do what I do best—shoot things."

She left it at that.

WHEN THE BELLY of the world grumbled, Elinor "Nellie" Watts knew that meant trouble, the kind of trouble you couldn't prepare for. Like any natural disaster—a tornado, a hurricane, an earthquake—you just had to make the best of it. And that was what any dinosaur attack was like. You did your best, kept your head down, and tried to stay out of sight.

As soon as Nellie watched the man from Washington leave the saloon, she knew they were in for it.

The town's sirens began to wail, signaling trouble ahead. Nellie wondered if these warning calls were necessary, and she sometimes thought they brought more danger to town than they did help. Beasts were attracted to noise, and the sirens made a whole lot of it. But alas, Oat Creek made their announcement to the good people who lived there and those who were just visiting, informing them they needed to secure a safe place and quickly, for there wasn't much time before the beasts would be upon them.

"We have to protect him," Nellie said, staring out the window, watching the shadows move among the night, the scared people of Oat Creek scrambling for cover. Some of them arrived inside the saloon, looking for the nearest table to climb under. The barkeep had already armed himself with the Winchester he'd kept under the register, and was now ducking behind the bar, peeking over the counter to make sure he didn't turn a blind eye to the action at hand.

The earth quivered again.

Getting closer.

"What do you mean?" Charlie asked. She was astounded by his stupidity, and suddenly wished for a partner with half a brain.

"I mean," she said, not hiding her agitation, "that if that man right there gets himself eaten or trampled, we lose that purse. He has the contracts and Washington doesn't. If he doesn't make it back in one piece, then we don't have any official deal."

Charlie didn't seem concerned about this aspect. "We'll just tell the president we signed the papers. He was the one who signed it originally. We'll be all right. So will old Smitty there. Got a feeling this ain't his first emergency situation. Washington has dinosaurs too, no?"

She'd never heard of any dinosaurs converging on the White House, but that didn't necessarily mean it had never happened.

"My suggestion," Charlie said, raising a fresh beer, "sit back, relax, and enjoy the show."

"You ain't scared?"

"Of what? We don't even know what we're dealing with yet."

And as he spoke those words, the world shook again, and this time, it wasn't from the approaching feet of some massive beast—it was the deafening roar that rattled the sky, the ground, the air and everything between.

Charlie set down his beer, looking like he never wanted to take another sip again. Sobered up real quick.

A faint smile drew her lips to one side, and Nellie asked, "Sure you ain't scared?"

He didn't answer, but he did reach for his revolver.

FROM THE LOOKOUT TOWER, Pip Downs continued to crank the siren. He hated doing so because the two massive beasts that patrolled the horizon didn't seem like they were coming this way at first. But rules were rules, and he was instructed to warn the town should he see any potential threat from the world's giant lizards or birds or whatever in tarnation they were. And the two creatures that seemed to be passing on through looked like big threats.

Tyrannosaurs. Two of them. A bull and cow, if Pip had to guess. Maybe on the hunt for food, looking to bring something back to their nest.

Pip couldn't tell for certain, but they sure looked like they had changed direction once he let out that warning. Headed right for them.

As they approached, he ducked in his tower, watching cautiously over the hip-high wall that provided some camouflage in the night. From what he'd learned in school, *Tyrannosaurs* were great night hunters, could see through the darkness as easily as a human could see the sky on cloudless afternoons. Had something to do with their eyes, the way they absorbed the darkness, but hell if Pip Downs could remember that particular lesson. All he knew was that the carnivores were just as dangerous in the dark as they were in the light, and that made Pip a wee bit nervous. He'd never been on duty during an episode. Hell, there hadn't been an attack on Oat Creek in going on six years. A few close calls but nothing to record in the town's history. Pip hoped to God that the two beasts were just passing through, seeing what they could scavenge from the back alleys, maybe kill a few cows locked up in the pens on the town's eastern border, but keep their visit short enough so no humans would die.

The *Tyrannosaurs* crossed the town's border, stalking the empty streets, their heads bobbing like giant turkeys, looking around, examining their surroundings, searching for their next feast. Pip unloaded his bladder in his skinnies, too scared to reach for the piss-bucket in the corner of the tower. As soon as he did so, the bull stopped. Craned his head back to the tower, its evil eye homing in on Pip. Pip locked eyes with the beast, and an audible, "No" escaped from him. Did the thing hear his piss hitting the clothing? Did it smell it? Pip didn't know. But he did know this—he was more screwed than a roaming alley cat in heat.

The bull turned back to the tower and lowered its massive head. It knew Pip was too high up, the top of the tower a good extra ten feet above the *Tyrannosaur's* snout, built specifically for reasons such as this. It didn't make Pip feel any better that he wasn't in danger of being snatched out of there. Mostly because the thing was determined to eat him, or at the very least, it was going to try.

Pip gripped the railing that bordered the tower's cockpit and held on for dear life. The bull swung its massive head into the tower's middle, the sheer force of the impact causing the wood and metal straps to give, and Pip watched the world tumble before him. He screamed, the noise an involuntary reaction to the horrific realization that he wasn't coming home tonight. Nor would he ever.

Pip's world went black the second the tower collapsed on the ground. At least he wasn't alive when the *Tyrannosaurs* dug him out of the debris with their snouts and divvied him up like the last biscuit at Thanksgiving dinner.

FROM THE SALOON'S front window, Charlie Archer watched the bull take down the watchtower in a single, effortless nudge. The feat was impressive, and he now knew the beasts were hunting —not scavenging—tonight. Hunting for themselves, for the nest they had left behind. In his experience, *Tyrannosaurs* were primarily scavenger types, not much for hunting. But sometimes desperation called, and the beasts had to do what they had to do in order stay atop the food chain.

"I'm going to check on our friend," Nellie said, releasing her twin revolvers from the leather holster's captivity.

"Don't go out there," Charlie warned. "Seriously. Those *Tyrannosaurs* are on the hunt, and they'll take anything they can get. Even a skinny little thing like you."

"What a compliment," she said, rolling her eyes. "That the best you got?"

"For the moment. Check back when I'm not a few blocks down from a couple of man-eating gargantuans."

"Come with me." She nodded at the small hotel across the way and slightly diagonal to their current position. Of course, they would have to travel *toward* the *Tyrannosaurs* in order to reach the establishment. But the mom and pop were currently occupied chewing on their first kill, crunching the town's lookout between their powerful jaws. Wouldn't be long before they finished and moved on to their next snack. The window of opportunity was closing and closing quickly. "Let's just make sure Smitty is all right. It'll put my mind at ease. And I'll track better knowing that the paperwork is in order."

"Can't see the sense in it."

She didn't seem to take offense to that statement. Instead, she continued to watch the two beasts devour their rewards. "I really need that money, Mr. Archer. I really do, and I don't think a man like you could understand."

"Need the money? I'd think a big celebrity gunfighter like you wouldn't need any."

"You'd be surprised."

And she was right about that—he was surprised. He thought she'd earned a pretty penny in those shootout tournaments, not to mention some of the bounties she collected on the side. She wasn't as prolific as he was in that department, but she'd made a name for herself among the bounty hunter community. Maybe she had a drug problem or an alcohol problem. Gambling? Shit, he could name at least ten in his inner circle who had at least one of those three. Most of them had at least two of those problems. It was common. Maybe she was in deep with some vicious, unforgiving sharks, and this coin from Washington was the only way out.

It was a hell of a lot of money.

Hell of a lot.

But Charlie saw past the dollar signs.

He only saw the name Francis Burner.

"All right," he said, giving up. Such was the way with Charlie Archer and beautiful women. "Let's see him through this, make sure he doesn't meet the teeth of our new friends."

"Thank you."

The two of them stood, and then headed out into the moonlit drag of Oat Creek.

FINN AMBLED out into the center of the street just as two shadows left The Oyster to do the same. His first thought was *no one could be this crazy, let alone two somebodies.* But here he was with two strangers, and he could see they were armed, each of them brandishing two revolvers. The man twirled one of them on his two centermost fingers. Finn made quick work of the addition, coming to the conclusion that their four and his two made six, and those numbers were slightly better than just his two, but still not enough to take down two full-grown *Tyrannosaurs,* unless they had brought with them an endless supply of ammo. He guessed that wasn't the case, though Finn *had* seen his fair share of weirdness. At the very least, a few bullets could potentially scare off the duo, force them to seek alternate dinner arrangements. That was the best they could hope for with just six guns.

He tipped his hat to the two strangers, and they nodded.

"Beautiful night out, huh?" Finn said, listening to the approaching growls.

"Be better if there wasn't thunder coming from below," the man said, stopping the gun from dancing on his fingertips, pointing it at the massive target lumbering through the center of town. The dinosaur kicked up statues of dust as it gained speed.

Finn gave the woman gunslinger a quick once over, which he almost always did when he saw a pretty woman. This one, however, was strapped with two revolvers, fine pieces, so fine he almost became jealous that they were better than the ones in his possession.

"Ma'am," he said. "You sure you know how to handle them thangs?"

She glared at him with cold eyes, eyes that have killed before, and the stony-gray look actually caused him to apologize. And Finn Hampton wasn't in the business of apologizing to no one. Not often anyways.

"Yes, ma'am. Sorry about that," he said with a brief chuckle, and then turned to the two *Tyrannosaurs.* They had gained speed, causing the ground to quake all around them. Finn heard things falling off walls and furniture crashing to the floors inside the surrounding buildings and apartments. "How much ammo y'all got?"

"Enough," the man whispered.

"Good."

The two *Tyrannosaurs* lumbered down the main drag, swinging their heads, looking out for killable sacks of meat, anything they could bring back to their kin. Finn brought up his guns, locking his elbows, ready to manage the recoil.

"Y'all ready?" Finn asked.

He heard the others drop their hammers, those harsh clicks, and they didn't need to verbally confirm anything—they let their guns do the talking for them, and before Finn could blink, their conversations started to fill the air, along with the sweet, savory scents of smoke, and lead, and blood.

CHARLIE WATCHED a piece of flesh rip free from the dinosaur's shoulder, a mark just left of the animal's stubby, stunted arm. If the things hadn't noticed them yet, they did now. The bullet couldn't have done much damage in the grand scheme of things —at twenty feet tall, the full-grown *Tyrannosaur* seemed barely affected. A bee sting in comparison. But it got the bull's attention, and the dinosaur stopped, turned, opened its maw, and treated the airwaves to the sound of its anger coming alive.

Charlie took this opportunity to unload his chambers, and he knew the others were waiting to make their moves. That was the best strategy in any gunfight, whether it be a rival gunfighter or a hungry carnivore—keep the shots coming. So after Charlie emptied his chambers into the *Tyrannosaur,* all but two bullets hitting the desired target, Nellie was next. While Charlie filled the chambers with more rounds, Nellie relieved hers, pumping her rounds into the cow. The firepower seemed to back her up, but then again, Nellie had landed all twelve shots. She was clearly the better shooter, not that Charlie would have doubted the claim had someone come right out and said it.

Once her chambers were spent, she went on and restocked, doing so more deftly than Charlie had, and he had to admit— the girl was putting him to shame. Not that he minded much. Some men, a thing like that might have driven them mad, having a girl be better at anything considered manly, *gun*play chief among those things. But Charlie didn't mind, not one bit. He didn't see women as inferior like some men did. Hell, *most.*

When Nellie was out and rapidly plugging those empty chambers, it was the newcomer's turn to take his shots, and he did so, more accurately than Charlie, hitting eleven of twelve, splitting six and six between the bull and the cow. The one bullet that missed did so by a curly tit hair, and only because the *Tyrannosaur* stumbled a little bit just as he had pulled the trigger. The last shot, however, was the crowning achievement of the entire exercise. The newcomer sunk a bullet right in the bull's left eye. The beast roared as one might think, an appropriate response to such an unfortunate incident, and the rage-filled explosion rattled the windows of every shop from the south end of town to the north. After that, it was Charlie's turn again. And so on and so forth, until the gunslingers were nearing the end of their supply. Charlie had told the newcomer that they had enough ammo, but he was beginning to think they most certainly did not.

But now, the *Tyrannosaurs* were starting to backpedal, and Charlie could see their shooting was having some effect. Bee stings or not, it was driving them back toward the south side of town. They weren't charging, which was good. Charlie had expected that maneuver, especially from the bull. He'd seen it before on the plains. Six wagons had come across a young bull and had started firing upon it, hoping to fell the beast and harvest the corpse for meat and skins, but the bull had charged and had taken the firepower head on. The wagons eventually brought the Tyrannosaur down, but not before the bull had wrecked three of the six wagons, and slaughtered at least twenty men. He'd been one of the lucky other three wagons that got to trundle home without a scratch.

That was nearly twenty years ago.

Things had changed a lot in twenty years.

But *Tyrannosaur* behavior more or less remained the same. And they were lucky that this bull was not as aggressive. Maybe that had to do with traveling with the cow, maybe because there was now a nest to go back to and it couldn't risk its life knowing there were young to provide for—some kind of paternal instinct not lost from species to species. The gesture made Charlie recall his own kin

(towering inferno, blackened bodies lying at the base of smoke-stacks that're filling the skies with ash)

and how he missed being a father.

"Pay attention!" the newcomer shouted at him, and Charlie snapped back to the moment, the now, the dark and the dinosaurs that threatened the town, his potential earnings provided by the United States of America.

He dug into his waist pouch and retrieved another three rounds, the last of his supply. Loading the chambers, he faced the bull. It was snapping at the air and trying to rub its wounded eye on the roof of the gun store. Roof shingles and siding boards came loose, and the shop owner, who'd probably been asleep inside, probably in the second-story apartment, came diving through the front window. He landed on the deck, near the shuffling feet of the bull. Cursing, screaming for his life, he scrambled to his knees, and then made one move toward the back alley.

The cow was on him. She nipped at his feet, knocking him to the ground. His body hit a puddle of mud with a loud wet sound, and then he was hoisted into the air by his right leg. She backed up and crouched down as if she expected more gunfire and wanted to make herself a smaller target. The bull continued to rub his put-out eye against the building, causing the roof to cave in. It snarled in a vexed combination of frustration and agony. The cow made a noise without opening its jaws, without risking the captured prey, something guttural that somehow reached even the three gunslingers, and got the bull thinking alternatively. The male dinosaur gave the gunfighters one last look with the good eye, and then turned to follow his bride out of town the way they had come.

The gun shop owner screamed all the way into the distance, across the desert, and the coyotes replied, their screeching howls echoing through the night.

"PRETTY GOOD WITH THEM GUNS," Finn said to the lady, but she did not respond. "Come on now, I apologized. Never judge a book by its cover. I know that now."

She continued to ignore him, and once the *Tyrannosaurs* were no longer visible and their footfalls no longer caused the town to shake, she spun away from him and his sweet talk.

"Park it, friend-o," Charlie said. "The lady isn't interested."

"Sorry. Didn't realize you two were an item."

At this Nellie reversed course, spinning on her heels like a child's top. "I ain't *nobody's* item." She stormed over to Finn and dug her forefinger into his chest. "Got that, pal?"

Finn surrendered, throwing his hands up. "Hey, I got it. Just never seen a woman shoot as good as you. Hell, being honest—I ain't seen no one shoot as good you."

"Well, ya seen it. Now fuck off back where you came from."

"I don't know—three of us—we made a pretty dynamic

squad. That kind of chemistry don't come around too often, and I was wondering...well, hell. I know who you are. Be lying if I said I didn't. You're Elinor Watts, ain't cha? And you—well, you're Charlie Archer. Name's Finn Hampton and it's a pleasure to—"

"Don't care what your name is," Nellie said, her tongue sharper than a knife prepped to cut buffalo meat. "Piss off or you might make me angry."

"I'd listen to her, friend," Charlie warned.

Finn looked at them. "I can take a hint, I suppose. Just wanted you to know that what just happened was one of the three most exciting things that's ever happened in my life, next to getting laid for the first time and—"

Nellie voiced her disgust with a crunchy breath, and then made her way over to the hotel.

"Was it something I said?" Finn asked.

Charlie smiled, clapped the man on the shoulder, and said, "Son, you done good tonight. Saved a lot of people from meeting their makers, I'm sure of it. Best stop there and get some rest."

"I guess so, but shit—didn't you feel it? The three of us. We make quite the trio."

Charlie smiled but didn't acknowledge the kid's comments. He waved lazily over his shoulder and followed Nellie to the hotel, where she was undoubtedly checking on Smitty to make sure he was completely intact and in peak condition to travel back east.

"Well, if y'all change your mind, I got an apartment just over..."

But they were gone.

And Finn Hampton was left in the middle of the dusty road, riding high on the adrenaline rush that had just conquered his body.

2
___

BURNER BAGS THE BEAKS * CHARLIE RIDES AGAIN *
BEAUTIFUL CREATURES * A SURPRISE ON THE
MOUNTAIN TRAIL * THE SKY HAS TEETH AND IT IS
HUNGRY

The wagons pull into town, all six of them, and the men riding are already liquored up, celebrating the big haul. The convoy made it back with no trouble at all, which is quite surprising to the entire crew on account of the last one going so disastrously. About a month ago, the caravan was attacked by a pack of raptors near the Blackhill Mountains. It was a terrible ordeal, and it set production back several weeks.

But this job went off fine, and as they roll into the small town of Highlow Grands, Billy-Boy Tanner jumps from the wagon, landing softly in the sandy earth below. His boots make an awful crunching sound, that quick snap of new leather, as they slam on the ground. The man doesn't feel the impact in his knees because he's pretty good and drunk. Doesn't feel much of anything, not that that's highly unusual for Tanner. He'll be the first one to tell you that he doesn't have much in the way of feelings, not since some bastard plucked out his eye all them years back. An event like that changes a man, and Billy-Boy Tanner was forever altered by that one traumatic moment.

The wagons slow to a halt, the horses neighing their appreciation for the eventual relief. Tanner moves to the back of the wagon and starts heaving off the collected sacks, the ones filled with the illegal cargo. He grunts at his associates, telling them they best get moving or there will be hell to pay, and hell might be a lump on the head or catching a bullet in the kneecap; the men have seen both from their second-in-command and neither action would surprise them one bit.

In about ten minutes the cargo is unloaded, resting in a pile near the corral, where a few horses run back and forth, getting in their daily dose of exercise. The Pteranodon wings are brought to the town's butcher where they will be chopped and sorted, prepared for a town-wide feast that everyone's invited to, hosted by the big man himself, the boss man, the man whose name you hear and immediately start to tremble from all the stories you done heard about him, all those terrible things he's done in his lifetime, some of them so outrageous and unbelievable that it's hard to consider the stories to be true. But Billy-Boy Tanner—he believes every word of them. Just looking into the evil bastard's dead-star eyes gives away a hint of the truth—he's done these things, and so much more, more than the world will ever truly know. Yep, dead-star eyes. That's just what they look like, exploded stars floating in an empty void of a galaxy that may have once been bright. Planets gone cold and forever dark. That's what it's like staring at the man, his eyes, and Billy-Boy Tanner does his best to look elsewhere when he faces him one-on-one.

Francis Burner.

The man in the black hood.

Just as he thinks he's going to avoid a conversation with the aforementioned son of a bitch, Tanner hears a slow clapping sound coming *from one of the houses back yonder the corral. Emerging from the spring-loaded hinged louvered doors, Burner himself makes an appearance out on the house's deck, the setting sun casting an obvious purple glow across his visage. Burner steps out clapping, his face concealed by that awful black hood, the only holes in the fabric being those little dots for him to see through. No space for his mouth or nose to take in air, and Tanner thinks that's okay because the man doesn't need to breathe, no sir.*

No, and that's because Francis Burner is a dead man come back to life, and dead men don't need no air.

Or so he believes. Can't be sure. Can't be sure about a lot, and Tanner isn't too sure. Maybe Burner never died in that train wreck, but then again, maybe he did. Maybe he's a ghost and all of this is crazy, and he's been consorting with a spirit these last few winters. Maybe Tanner's just gone crazy and lost his mind and there is no Francis Burner at all, and this thing in the black hood is a figment of his imagination and it's really been Tanner organizing and plotting this whole operation from the start.

Wouldn't that be a hoot.

But no—it's real. All of it. Burner is back from whatever hell he rose from, and he's here to do the devil's work, and the devil's work is great for Tanner's pockets, so he ain't complaining none.

"Well done, Billy-Boy," Burner announces to the gathering before him. His voice is so deep and dark that just hearing it for the first time in a long time is enough to lay Tanner's bones in a bed of ice. "Your success pleases me."

"Well, I aim to please, Burner. That's what I'm here for." Tanner hates the way he sounds when he's speaking to Burner—makes him sound weak and inferior in front of the other men. Which he is, but he doesn't like it all the same. "Count about fifty on this haul. Figure we can rest up a couple days and then head back, grab another fifty and—"

"Tomorrow," Burner says, interrupting. "Tomorrow at dawn."

"*Uh, say what now?*" Tanner is confused. *He couldn't possibly mean to ride back out tomorrow morning, not after just getting back home. These men need to rest up, need to gather their wits about them, relax their bones, their minds. They need to eat well, drink away the aches and pains, and, if possible, fuck them away too.*

"*I don't believe I stuttered,*" Burner says. "*Tomorrow at dawn, you'll ride back to the Canyon and bring the beaks of another fifty birds.*"

"*Sir...*"

"*Sir what?*"

"*With all due respect, the men need their rest. It's a grueling trip to the Canyon, and even though this was a much smoother operation than the previous one...well, we need a break is all.*"

"*Sleep tonight. Leave tomorrow.*"

"*Sir, the men, the crew, we can't expect—*"

"*Find new men. New crew.*"

This advice doesn't come as much of a shocker. "*Sir, even if I could, the horses—*"

"*Find new horses.*"

Tanner can't help it. He laughs. Probably shouldn't have done it, but it's either that or scream, tantrum, or act out in some violent manner, and he figures Burner won't forgive those latter options.

"*Burner,*" *he starts, knowing he should shut his mouth before putting his thoughts out there for everyone to hear, but then again, that just isn't like Billy-Boy Tanner. Nope. Not one bit. His mouth and thoughts have been colluding against him for ages, always getting him into nasty situations—like, losing a goddamn eye situations.* "*I can't stress enough how tired these men are. Horses too. I want to ride back out to the Canyons just as much as you, I swear it I do, but...it's just not smart.*"

Burner only glares at him, those dead-star eyes wandering into the depths of Tanner's soul. He can feel him rooting around in there, like a life-threatening winter sickness that burrows itself deep in the lungs. Breaking him down. Dissecting him.

Then he turns, scanning the gathering of men. "This how you all feel?" he asks. "You all feel you need to rest more? Days upon days upon days?"

Tanner doesn't think telling him that a few days isn't all that much, and however far behind they are, a few days ain't gonna set them back none. He doesn't dare say that.

No one, of course, speaks their mind. Instead, they look around the ranch, the town, the purpling sky, and the shadows crawling across the mountain range. They don't dare look into those dead stars for eyes.

"No one else seems to have a problem with it, Tanner," says Burner, much too calmly for Tanner's nerves.

"That's because they are too terrified to speak their minds."

"And you are not?"

This is a ploy, possibly Burner's intent the entire time.

"Fear is a luxury I cannot afford, sir."

"Fair enough. I actually appreciate you standing up for these spineless mutants. Make a fine leader, you do, and that's why I like keeping you around, Billy-Boy Tanner."

"I appreciate your confidence, sir."

"But you will leave tomorrow at first light and we will speak no more of it." At this, Burner flexes his shoulders, and his neck, as if this is a quick-draw challenge and he's loosening his muscles, getting them ready for the draw.

But this isn't a gunfight. It's not a fight at all.

Tanner knows he has no option. It's this or quit and die.

"I understand," Tanner says, nodding.

"Good. Because I'd really hate to see you lose that second eye. It'd be an awful thing, to be completely blind. Wouldn't it?"

With this last piece of rhetoric, Burner heads back inside the establishment, a few of his closest goons following in tow.

There's a brief moment where everyone else just stands there, not sure how to carry on. A horse neighs, flicking the flies nearing its bunghole. In the distance the wolves are calling for the moon. And somewhere close, Billy-Boy Tanner can hear the beating of his own heart.

"What're y'all standing around for?" he barks. "Get some sleep. You heard the man—we head out at dawn."

THERE WAS ALWAYS a special sensation when Charlie Archer rode out on a new hunt, and he'd always attributed this to the excitement of the fresh chase. The way his heart clicked in his chest was different, and it was different each time. A new hunt, a new feeling, but exhilarating just the same. And now he had someone to hunt with, which brought a whole new level to the bounty game.

Last night's twirl with the two *Tyrannosaurs* was still fresh in his mind, and he had a feeling that some of those good sensations were the result of that win. But there was something else stirring in his chest, a feeling he had tried so desperately to ignore, one that had showed up rarely over the last seven years or so, one he never engaged in when it did crop up so unexpectedly.

He glanced over at Nellie, watching the wind blow her hair

around in wild directions. The sun brightened her face, and she closed her eyes, soaking in the warmth of the new light. The air smelled better up here near the mountains, and their trek so far had been filled with magical sights, storybook images he wished he had some way of capturing so he could reflect back on them with crystal clarity sometime later, when he was an old man and sitting near a fireplace, remembering all those crazy things he had done when he was younger. Majestic sights that were hard to describe, the kind you had to be there for to experience the fullness of its beauty.

They passed a hot spring where a gaggle of *Hadrosaurs* were hanging out, basking in the clear, steamy water. The dinosaurs paid them no attention, and the two rode past, toward their destination without any fuss. Charlie worried about taking the mountain trails on account of that was where the raptors and other apex predators liked to lay their eggs, but this time of year, nearing so close to winter, he didn't think it would be much of a problem. Nests were rare this season, and most of the carnivores had already begun to migrate south. Still, didn't mean they weren't here and weren't somewhat active.

"You like the mountain trails?" he asked Nellie, trying to strike up a conversation to pass the time. They'd been quiet these last few miles, and, if he was being honest, he'd grown a little bored. There was only so much scenery one could take in, even if the sights were gorgeous and the leaves were changing from their summer greens into something fiery and burnt. When she didn't respond right away, he followed up with, "I like the mountain trails. Especially this season. Something beautiful about the death of summer."

They took their horses from a gallop to a walk, giving the beauties the opportunity to rest and catch their breath.

"You don't like to talk much, do you?" he asked her.

She didn't make eye contact with him, not even for a second. Nellie kept her focus front and center on the trail that careened through the mountainside, the trees flanking their path, dropping their dead leaves all round them.

"What's there to talk about?" she asked. "Seasons? Seasons bore me, Mr. Archer. Almost as much as the weather bores me."

"Well, what excites you then?" Now she looked at him, and he hated the look that crossed her features. He suddenly realized that she might have misinterpreted his question. "Oh, I didn't mean anything like that. Honest."

"What do you want from me, Mr. Archer?" The question shocked him. There wasn't anything he wanted from her, and he combed back over their previous conversations, looking for the part where he might have suggested he had. "What is it you're after on this trip?"

"Sorry, I don't catch your meaning. I'm just out to do a job, just like you. Figured since we were gonna be stuck with each other for at least a fortnight, that we could be friendly with each other. If you want me to shut my flapper, just tell me so and it will be done."

She seemed to give the option some thought. "No, I'm sorry. I just...my experience with men on the road has not been a pleasant one, and I'm afraid I've judged your intentions on the basis of others."

"Well, shit. That's okay, I guess."

"You're not offended?"

"Offended?" He slapped invisible flies. "Hell no. Not like you went pissing on my momma's grave or something like that."

"Have you ever done that? Pissed on someone's grave, I mean?"

Charlie didn't have to think about that one too hard. "Once, actually."

"Really?" She giggled.

"Yeah, I was drunk and the man whose grave it was owed me about two hundred dollars in poker debt. Son of a bitch probably deserved more than a pissing, but it was about all I could offer up at the time, 'cept for digging him up and choking his skeleton. That seemed like a lot of work, though. Pissing wasn't all that hard, even in that condition."

She seemed to enjoy that short tale and continued to smile. They both went quiet for the next mile, but not without trying to start a new conversation. Small talk that quickly petered out, went nowhere. It wasn't until the mountain trail took them down to a shallow valley, the bottom of a green pasture where herds of *Triceratops* and *Sauropods* lumbered and grazed that they spoke again. It was a marvelous sight; one Charlie Archer couldn't get enough of. Sure he'd seen his fair share of dinosaurs, especially the friendly and indifferent kinds, but something about seeing them this close was always something he marveled over. Their massive forms, beautiful creations that had existed on this planet way longer than humans had, if you were to believe the scientists. If you were to believe the pastors, they'd tell you God created dinosaurs and men at the same time, and that the two species were designed to co-exist with one another, like any good planetary cohabitants. Like any animals.

"God, they're beautiful, aren't they?" Charlie said, staring perhaps too fondly.

"I guess," she said, "when they're not trying to eat you."

"Oh, these are herbivores. Won't eat you."

She rolled her eyes at him. "You think I can't tell the difference? Did my twelve years of schooling, and I know my dinosaurs."

He nodded in some vague, apologetic way. "Well, anyway. These we can admire for a while. If you want."

"We can't. We have a job to do." She scanned the bright sky, the position of the sun. "Not much daylight left. Gonna have to make camp somewhere up yonder, on that ridge." Gesturing with her chin up, she pointed to the spot previously referenced.

"Yeah, figure that. Can we just stay and watch them graze a little longer?"

Smiling, she asked, "You really enjoy these animals, don't you?"

"Something about the ones that aren't trying to eat you calms me a bit." He let out a deep sigh and then dipped into his satchel for his tobacco. After he rolled a cigarette, he offered the bag of brown shavings to Nellie, who declined without needing to waste a single second on the decision.

"Disgusting."

"Not a smoker?"

"What gave it away? The fact I used the word *disgusting*?"

He grinned foolishly as he lit up. "You got a real standoffish vibe going for you. You know that?"

"Been practicing it all my damn life."

"Why's that?"

Nellie shrugged. "Way I am, I guess."

"What do you need the money for?"

She snapped her head in his direction while backing up her horse in order to avoid the wafting second-hand smoke. "Excuse me?"

"You heard." A chimney's worth of smoke billowed from his spreading smile.

"None your damn business, that's what."

"Come on. We ain't got a whole lot to talk about on the trail, and I think it might make for an interesting conversation."

She pulled her horse away from the edge of the valley and headed up the trail, toward the ridge above them.

"Hey now!" Charlie called after her. She didn't respond, not that he had expected her to. Snuffing out the lit smoke on his bootheel, he prepped his gelding, gripping the reins and putting his free spur into his ribs, and then set off after her.

She didn't stop, didn't slow down, and it took a good quarter hour before she slowed down again, allowing him to catch up.

"I'm sorry," he said. "Didn't mean to offend. Just trying to be friendly, that's all."

She continued her tight-lipped approach, not that he expected her to spill the beans on her financial situation, her reasons for needing the change so badly.

"Forgive me?"

A sideways glance. It was something. Not much of something, but something, nonetheless.

"Look, I'll make it up to you—no more asking about the money and what you'd use it for, and I'll even hunt you some rabbits tonight. You like rabbit stew?"

The way her tongue touched the edge of her lips, he knew she liked rabbit stew, liked it very much.

"I like rabbit stew," she confirmed about five seconds later.

"Excellent. Rabbits it is."

As promised, Charlie delivered on the rabbit stew. He'd found a warren not more than a half mile from their camp, stalked it for about a half hour, and came back with four full-grown rabbits. The can of soup he'd had stuffed in his satchel made for a fine base, and sometime after nightfall, after the stars bled through the sky and joined the moon in their nightly performance, the pair sat down on logs they'd dragged over to their fire and ate in steady silence. After they were finished and had washed their faces and mouths in a nearby stream, they returned to the logs to do a bit of stargazing.

"Ever wonder what's up there?" Charlie asked.

"All the time," she answered, and her response somewhat surprised Charlie. He didn't peg her as the type who'd ponder the secrets of the universe, what lived beyond the stars and the giant curtain that hung over the world.

"Like, think there're other planets with people like us on them?"

She shrugged. "I mean, other planets obviously. Not sure there any like ours, though."

"I think there're other places out there like this. With people that look exactly like us. And somewhere out there, they're sitting around wondering the same thing, asking the same questions—anyone else out there?"

"It's interesting to think about," she mused, and sipped on the hot tea she'd made. "It's getting late. Figure I should turn in. We gotta long ride tomorrow."

He nodded, watching the glow from the fire wash her face in tangerine shadows.

"Don't look at me like that," she said to him.

"Look at you like what?"

"You know what."

"I assure you, I don't."

"We sleep separately, Mr. Archer."

His hands rose as if something had been hurled in his direction and his natural instinct was to catch it. "Now, now. I ain't got an impure thought in my head."

"Good. See that it stays that way. Empty of impurities." With that she got up from the log and tossed out what was left of her tea. "Good night."

"Good night, Nellie."

Before she left, they heard something in the woods somewhere behind them. They spun toward the sound, hearing the snapping of branches and crunching of plants beneath the boots of some unexpected presence.

Both went to their holsters.

"Stop!" Charlie said, raising his gun toward the approaching sounds.

A shadow froze, the dark silhouette remaining far enough away from the light. Charlie couldn't identify him. Or her. But he freed his gun, his instincts taking over, letting him know it wasn't normal for people to be wandering around at this hour, out on the mountain trail. Usually that meant someone was in trouble. Maybe their horse had died, or a wagon took on a bum tire. Either way, Charlie wasn't much in the mood to deal with other people's problems, not when he had a head full of his own.

"Identify yourself," Charlie demanded of the figure.

"Name's Tucker. Tucker Jones." The voice was small and weak, sounding much younger than he would have expected, not that he had much evidence to suspect otherwise. "I...shit, my family is in trouble, mister."

Charlie kept his revolver out just in case, but the worry in the kid's voice made the claim sound genuine. "What happened?"

"Got attacked about a mile back. Wagon jumpers. Whole lot of them. They came so fast..."

"Raptors?" asked Charlie, scanning the available darkness,

looking for iridescent eyes hiding in the brush. Raptors harbored a fair amount of intelligence, and, if the boy's story proved itself to be true, he wouldn't put it past a pack to leave one survivor to follow in hopes of it leading them to more prey. He'd seen them hunt like this before, and, as the seconds grew old, he suddenly was overcome with the notion to move off the mountain trail and into the valley. Better to risk being trampled than gobbled up in their sleep.

"Are they headed this way?" Charlie asked.

The boy stepped closer to the pale firelight. "I don't know. But mister? Ma'am? My family needs help. Still a chance to save them. The pack, they moved on and my daddy and mommy and little sister are trapped beneath the wagon."

Charlie scanned the horizon. Then he glanced over at Nellie, who returned his gaze. Both shared the same cautious expression, both hesitant to buy the boy's story at face value.

"Son, it's too dark out." What he wanted to say is, *"Boy, you're a liar. No pack hunter leaves a tipped wagon behind, not without extracting a meal from that tipped wagon. Either your family is dead or you're making the whole thing up, and in either case we cannot help you."*

But he didn't say those things, not yet. He wanted to keep the boy talking, let the truth reveal itself over time.

"But...my family?"

"Odds are," Nellie said, chiming in for the first time since the boy showed himself, "they're already dead."

The boy's eyes bounced between them, and when he finally figured out that his weak story wouldn't get any play here, he put his hands on his hips and said, "Oh, hell. They weren't buying that story anyway. And y'all's in position, no?"

"What—?" Before Charlie could process that question, he felt something cold press against his cheek, and it only took him about three seconds to figure out it was the barrel of a Colt, and that he was assuredly gonna die.

"Gotcha," said a hoarse whisper in his ears, with breath that smelled like dead rabbits.

"SAW you in that warren hunting for rabbits," the man said, pissing right there in front of them, not bothering to hide the deed or the weapon from which he shot the piss. He was a tall, dirty man who looked like he hadn't bathed since the Civil War. There were two other men surrounding their little camp—one of them was the boy who'd been a decent enough actor to pull off this little charade, and the other a shorter, rotund feller who didn't say much, but giggled every time the tall man spoke. Charlie figured he'd been shorted some brains at birth or something of the like. "Saw you hunting *my* warren for rabbits, if I may be so bold to say it."

"Didn't see your name etched in the soil above them," Charlie said plainly and without worry. "I apologize for my carelessness. Can we strike a truce?"

The tall man grinned as he tucked himself back into his pants. "I don't do truces, unfortunately for you."

"That is unfortunate."

The tall man glared at him, then burst out laughing. The giggler and the actor joined him, hooting and hollering. "Shit," the man said. "Usually by this point, our quarry would be begging for their lives! Don't shoot me, mister! Please, oh God! We'll do anything!" He slapped his knee as if these previous interactions were some of the funniest stuff alive. "You wouldn't believe the things people offer us in exchange for sparing their lives."

"Again, I apologize for my improper reaction to this current situation," Charlie said, feeling his faint grin slipping. "I wasn't under the impression our lives were at risk."

"Oh no?" the tall man said, amused. "What do you think we're doing here?"

Charlie looked around at the three men. "Well...I guess I thought you were friendly mountain folk looking for a place to stay warm, and, well, shit—well, my wife and I were just going to invite you over for a fireside chat. Hell, she was just about to tell a spooky ghost story. You like ghost stories, mister?"

At this, the tall man scowled. "No, I don't like fucking ghost stories." He grabbed his revolver and waved it around threateningly. "What kind of ploy is this?"

"No ploy. Just a couple of traveling folk who like to tell ghost stories in the dark." Charlie patted the space on the log next to him. "Come. Have a listen."

The boy looked at Charlie with a certain level of disgust, and Charlie prided himself on this small accomplishment, a mischievous grin spreading across his face.

The tall man leaned over and pressed a finger to his chest. "Do you know who the fuck I am?"

"No, sir. Can't say I do. Sure are a tall feller, though. Lemme guess. You get to place the little angel atop the Christmas tree come every December."

The tall man didn't seem to appreciate this joke. He spat on Charlie's boots.

"My name is Chester McClellan, leader of the McClellan Three."

Charlie perked up at this noise. "You...you're Chester? Chester McClellan?"

"Got wax in your ears, boy? That's what I done said."

"Well, shit. Good to meet you. Been looking for you boys for a long time now. Glad we finally get to meet face to face."

"And who the hell might you be?"

"Name's Charlie Archer."

"Charlie...Charlie Archer?" It looked like he'd just heard a ghost story and the very mention of ghosts conjured forth some spectral image before him. "Well, fuck me side-saddled. If it ain't the great Charlie Archer. Huh, I guess that is you. You look a lot worse than I imagined. Would you believe it, boys? The best bounty hunter this side of Texas. What are the odds?"

"Oh, probably about the same as getting impaled by a *Stegosaur* spike. But you know—small world and all of that."

"Well, this is a pickle," McClellan said, tipping his hat with the barrel of his revolver. "A pickle indeed."

"We should kill them," the boy said, Cletus, as Charlie had heard of them. The other one must have been Willy. He was surprised he hadn't pieced together the trio from the start, but the darkness, given what it was, and the unexpectedness of how the whole sham went down, he didn't beat himself up too badly about the slip. "We should kill them and leave them for the carnivores."

"Oooh," Chester McClellan said. "That sure is a sound i-dear."

"Kill 'em!" Willy said, sounding like his mouth was full of marbles. "Kill 'em! Kill 'em!"

"Oh, don't worry, Willy!" Chester said. "We gonna kill 'em pretty good, that's for goddamn sure. But this one..." He focused on Nellie, working his feet in her direction. "This one we might have a little fun-zees with first. Ain't that right, darling?"

"Depends on what your idea of fun is, you worthless, backwoods, rat-faced cousin-fucker," she replied sharply.

"Well, looksee the mouth on you. Tsk, tsk. Pretty little lady shouldn't cuss so much, methinks."

"Methinks you take that two-inch pecker you just had out and go fuck a chicken. That's about the only action you'll be getting tonight, I guarantee it."

"Oh, I'm sorry. You seem to be confused. See, I wasn't asking anything from you. I was telling you what I'm gonna take."

"Cute," she said, smiling. "But if you're thinking of trying anything sinful, I'll kill you dead."

At this, Chester burst out laughing. The knee-slapping variety. Charlie wished the bastard dead and buried right there, but wishing was one thing and doing was another, and right now he didn't have his guns at his disposal—Willy had fetched them and hidden them somewhere on his person.

"Oh, girl," Chester said, getting in his last guffaws. "You funny. But we got your guns! And there ain't nowhere to go. Plus, up here on the mountain trail, ain't no one gonna hear you scream." His eyes turned sharp and bitter as if he could see the impending violence with such crystal clarity, and what he saw there excited him and terrified him all at once. "And you will scream for me. They always do."

The next thing that happened came as quite a shock to everyone involved—first, the sound of the world cracking in half, an explosion of sorts. Then there was the sudden puncture that opened up on Chester McClellan's chest, a scarlet flower blooming forth, and the startled look in his eyes that reminded Charlie of the rabbits he had hunted earlier. The way they looked moments before they knew they would become a fine stew.

"Well, fuck me in the—"

The next puncture opened up on his forehead, dislodging a chunky spray of blood and brain matter, the viscous slop splashing into the fire, causing the flickering flames to hiss like an agitated rattler. And then the strength must have fled his body because Chester McClellan swayed forward like the lead actor in some stage play trying to visually capture the emotion of falling in love for a pretty girl, except Chester wasn't in love, far from it.

Chester was dead; on his feet though, as if his body didn't know it yet.

Cletus's eyes immediately scanned the hills, looking for the mysterious shooter, hoping to pick up a shadow in all that darkness, but the cover of night was far better than the boy's eyesight. He was too slow, and the next slug popped his head like a festering pimple, the brain juice ejecting out the back of his skull, traveling into the dark unknown behind him. He was way dead before his body collapsed on the dirt, entering that eternal nap nobody had ever come back from, least not to Charlie Archer's knowledge.

Willy made a grunt, more of an amused sound, and Charlie knew immediately the boy didn't comprehend everything that had just transpired. Nor would he ever.

Before the bullet could come for him, Charlie jumped in front of the last remaining McClellan, waving his hands in the air and shouting unintelligible demands.

The bullet didn't come.

"Show yourself!" Charlie said. "Please!"

About three seconds later, the outline of a gunslinger appeared up near the ridge, looking down at the three living beings. Charlie thought it might have been an angel from the heavens, or maybe something else—one of those mysterious beings from the sky he was always thinking about, the ones that might live on a planet close to the one they call Earth. But as the figure dismounted the darkness, he noticed it was no interplanetary visitor, and certainly no angel.

"You," Charlie said.

"Me," Finn Hampton said, blowing away smoke from the barrel of his six-shooter.

"Aw, hell. No need to thank me," Finn said after a few seconds of silence from the two (seemingly ungrateful) survivors. Three if you counted the giggler, and Finn did incorporate his rescue and subsequent sparing into the mix. "Unless you want to."

"What the hell were you doing up there?" Nellie asked. "Were you...following us?"

"I might have been doing that." He shrugged. "Might have."

"You son of a—"

Charlie Archer stepped in front of her. "What the hell is going on, Finn? Why you following us?"

Finn looked at their two questioning stares as the flickering firelight painted their faces with a dim mango glow. "Guess it can't hurt to tell y'all the truth, huh? All right, all right. But first, what do we do about that big fella right there?"

Charlie half-turned back to Willy McClellan. The portly chap picked a scab under his right eye and then examined the dark flakes under his fingernail, looking like he might take a taste of the crusty remains. Then he did take a taste. Nibbling away on the knob that was his right forefinger, Willy looked out across the skies seized by nighttime's darkened touch and muttered, "*Kill 'em, kill 'em good now,*" as if he didn't know exactly what those words meant or why he was saying them. Just repeating what he'd heard out of some rhythmic routine. Almost ritualistically, a thing said on occasion to calm the nerves or fill a long silence. Spoken without any intent or distinction. Could have been any combo of words he'd repeated, just so happened to be those, and maybe that was because he'd heard them often. The McClellans were awful people, and they'd done a lot of killing. Finn had heard his fair share of stories regarding the trio and their wicked deeds.

"We can't leave him out here. He'll be dinosaur food," Charlie said. "There was a village about ten clicks back, maybe less. Someone there might be able to take him in temporarily, or better yet—find him a fitting home."

"That's banking on there's a soul generous enough in that town to do such a thing." Finn glanced at the kid with pity.

"Well, I think you should be the one to take him there and find out."

"Me?" Finn scoffed. "Why would I do a thing like that?"

Charlie pointed to exhibit A and exhibit B. "Well, considering you blew gaping holes in both his kin, leaving him an orphan, I'd say it's your responsibility."

Finn opened his mouth to respond, then closed it. "Shit."

"Yep," Charlie said, patting him on the back. "And do me a favor when you get there—stay put, yeah? Well, you don't have to stay there precisely, but don't follow us any longer. Okay?"

"I talked to that Washington fella back in Oat Creek," Finn finally blabbered.

"Smitty?" Charlie said with a scoff. "What's he got to do with this?"

"Well, I escorted him to his train, saw him off on account of him being scared after that run-in with the two *Tyrannosaurs*. Was able to earn a couple bits for my troubles. On the way there, he told me about what you two were up to at *Pteranodon* Canyon. I was able to smooth-talk him, squeeze some information out of him. Turns out, you two are looking for my old boss."

Charlie's throat bobbed. "You worked for Francis Burner?"

Finn waved the claim aside. "No, not that one. Tanner. Billy-Boy Tanner. Mean son of a bitch. He owes me more than a few dollars for some business we had awhile back. Tried to kill me over it, can you believe it? And well, I never got to collect that change, so I offered to help bring him in, that was, after I convinced Mr. Smitty from Washington that you two would need an extra gun, that however many men you think Tanner has in his employment, it's probably triple that. Maybe quadruple."

"We don't need your help," Nellie told him with utter confidence.

"I bet you believe that," Finn shot back. "But the truth is, Tanner has a following. You'd think a man like that wouldn't employ many friends, but if you did think that you'd be wrong. Might be why Francis Burner hired him in the first place, that and he has a reputation for getting things done." Finn's eyes drifted back to Willy, the boy who hardly seemed to care that both of his brothers' brains were leaking through holes in the center of their heads. Hardly cared at all. "Part of me thinks that Tanner is really running the whole operation and Burner is just a cover. Subterfuge. But I'm not sure Tanner is that smart. He's more of a do'er, not a thinker. Know what I mean?"

Charlie nodded. Nellie faced the available darkness, acting as if she was only present because there was nowhere else to go. If it had been daylight out, Finn thought she'd rather ride a hundred miles away from them than engage in this kind of talk. He couldn't figure her out but knew she didn't like him much.

"Ma'am," he said, turning to her. "Not sure what it is I did to offend you, but I assure you—I'm a good man and I want to help."

She snapped her head in his direction. "You're not getting a cut of our goddamn pay."

"No, ma'am. I worked out a separate deal with Smitty. Your purse remains the same." He put his hands out like, *See? How good of a deal is that?* "So you got the best of both worlds it seems. An extra gun—well, two—and you get to keep your pay on top of it."

"Stellar."

"We still have to take care of the kid," Charlie said, nodding over his shoulder at Willy. "Won't sleep too well knowing he ain't safe."

Finn nodded. "I'll ride him back into that town you spoke of, provided you draw me up some direction. Then I'll catch back up with y'all in a day or two. Ride by night to make up the difference." He checked the skies. "Still got a few hours of dark left. Might be able to get there by sunup."

"Well giddy up then, cowboy," Nellie said before leaving the campfire and the two dead bodies, and heading over to the makeshift tent a few paces away.

"What's up her keister?" Finn asked Charlie once she was gone. Clearly she could still hear everything that was being said, so Finn promised himself he wouldn't say anything he wouldn't say to her face. "I mean, I'm a nice guy. Real nice. I just want to help. Sure, I have some personal stake in taking out Tanner and the coin is nice, but really—we made a good team back in Oat Creek. I just want to be friendly is all."

Charlie patted him on the shoulder. "Maybe she'll warm up to you, cowboy."

"All right, fair enough. Look, I'm going to take the boy into town. Y'all rest up and I'll catch up with you over the next day. I ride real fast and my horse is as healthy as a...well, a horse, I guess."

"Fair enough."

"Draw me that map?"

Charlie tipped his cap. "After you help me haul these bodies far enough from camp to where they won't attract predators—then, aye, I'll draw you a map."

LIKE HE SAID HE WOULD, Finn caught up with them within the next day, before the next nightfall, and Charlie wondered how fast he'd ridden to pull off this surprising accomplishment. Charlie was no good at math—basic arithmetic was about all he could handle—but calculating time and distance was something he'd gotten pretty good at. And what disturbed him was that he couldn't make this simple equation work in his head. Finn would have had to ride into that town before morning and beat on every door, wake up every soul, and be lucky enough to find someone to take in the boy without asking too many questions, or any questions at all really. The math and the miles didn't allow for many questions, but even if he had managed one or two, it still didn't explain the quickness in which he returned. It wasn't like he had a pouch full of magic fairy dust he'd sprinkled all over his horse to help it sprout wings. Many strange and wonderful things happened in the west, but flying horses was pushing it.

When prompted about these calculations, Finn just said, "The town was closer than you mapped out is all."

Though the answer didn't soothe Charlie's suspecting mind, it was left at that.

That night, Charlie checked his map, saw there was a small town up near the Utah-Colorado border that had rooms available to rent. Usually those rooms were rented by the hour and usually those rooms had a woman stocked inside who also made an hourly wage by doing things that would turn God's cheeks several shades of raspberry. But Charlie figured the establishment would cut them a nightly rate and remove the woman from the bill, long as they paid in cash, and the per diem Smitty had given them was more than enough, or so he thought.

Once they arrived, Charlie couldn't ignore the eerie silence they walked into. If he didn't know any better (and he didn't, not really), he'd have said the town was run by ghosts. A haunted town out west wasn't entirely rare—he'd run across a few abandoned towns in his travels. Places that had caught a sickness, some sort of isolated plague, and the survivors had picked up and left in fear of catching the deadly disease. Left and never returned. When Charlie had arrived at these places, they usually stunk of the rotted dead. Usually saw rats the size of small dogs scurrying about, occupying the back alleys and houses that harbored the eroding corpses that would never be claimed by loved ones. Corpses left to become one with the rot.

But not this place. This place reeked of something else. It stunk with the *fresh* dead; the air smelled like new silver bullets straight from a gunsmith's workshop.

It didn't take long to stumble upon what had taken place here. The first body was crumpled in the middle of the road, a man's body with the head missing, a trail of gore snaking out from the opened neck, revealing the top of the man's vertebrae. No telling what had happened to his *cabeza,* only that it wasn't here, and the culprit had taken the head as a souvenir.

Trotting on, they discovered more bodies. Some of them hanging off hitching posts, some lying in water troughs, some looking like they were napping drunk in the center of the road. It wasn't until Charlie looked up and saw bodies on the roofs that he realized what must have happened here—the town had been attacked. By tall things.

Monsters.

"Well, shiiiiiit," Finn said, surveying the town now marked by the red touch of death. "What the hell did all this?"

Movement from somewhere close, and the sound of some material dragging across packed sand caught Charlie's attention. His eyes followed the movement, and he hopped off his horse, drawing his weapon and pointing it toward the sound. After his eyes adjusted to the pre-dusk glow, pushing back some of the obscurities resting in shadows up yonder, he saw what was causing the noise. Someone was pulling themselves across the ground, looking for cover, refuge from the thing that had torn through here. *Or things.*

In any case, someone was alive. And that someone needed help.

Charlie kept his weapon free out of habit, and with this many dead bodies around him he couldn't afford to be too lax. He made his way over to the survivor, asking his two partners to hold back with a raise of his fist. He approached the fountain in the center of town and walked around the outer rim, gaining a better look at this unfortunate crawler. Charlie thought he'd be better off dying like the rest of them, and only one good look at what remained told him that much. The man—a priest, he could now see—was missing one arm, the limb ripped free from the shoulder, making him look like an angry child's mangled plaything. An awful lot of blood soaking into the sand followed behind him.

Charlie stood over the priest and dropped to one knee. The man was trembling, mumbling some nonsense to himself, hardly paying any attention to the shadow falling around him— Charlie's shadow—and Charlie half-wondered if the man thought he was the reaper finally come to escort him off this mortal coil.

"Sky..." the priest mumbled; the only word Charlie could make out in that unintelligible rant. "Teeth."

"Sky teeth?" Charlie asked. "I don't follow you, padre. Perhaps you want to start over and articulate yourself a little better."

Charlie's suggestion seemed to go unheard as the priest continued to spew his near-nonsense. Charlie was able to make out a syllable here and there, but the broken words between them were without context and the entire message was lost in the nutter's speech.

"Padre, what would you like me to do?" He bit his lip, surveying the damage to the man's body. There were holes in his black button-down, pockets where the flesh had been ripped away. Dark tunnels of absent muscle, drilled all the way down to the bone. An ordinary citizen would have had trouble staring at the wounds for more than a few seconds, but Charlie was far from ordinary. His eyes lingered over the cuts and bruises that had already begun to bloat. "I hate to see a man suffer, but on the other hand I'd feel mighty awful about putting a man of the cloth out of his misery. Something about that certainly sits askew."

"Sky..." the priest said, ceasing his efforts. Slowly, he glanced back, over his shoulder, locking eyes with Charlie's curious gaze. "Sky. Sky. Sky. SKY."

"Heard you the first time, padre, but—"

"SKY." The preacher's hand jutted into the sky, a single raised finger pointed at the thing that had caused him and the town so much trouble.

Charlie turned just in time to avoid being flown down on. He rolled out of the way as the beast, no bigger than a small dog, hit the ground, flapping its wings furiously, squawking with a hungry rage that outmatched its size. The wings were bat-like, like that of your typical *Pterosaur,* but its head was stubby and canary-esque. More bird than lizard. Two perfect circles on each side of its head, blacker than any night Charlie had ever stargazed upon. A bright-orange beak, sloped to an angry angle like a sharp pair of scissors. Once the creature realized that (of the two) Charlie was the more difficult target, it quickly spun on the fallen preacher, hopping into the air and landing precisely on the faithful man's chest. The man screamed in abject horror as the bird immediately went for his eyes, the orange beak pecking and working so quickly that the orange flashed and blurred before it became wet with red.

Charlie watched with half fascination, half terror as the thing dug out the preacher's eyeballs, gobbling them up like soft grapes. Charlie wondered how the priest lived through the trauma, how his body hadn't spared him from the pain and allowed him to pass out yet. He prayed that a swift, comfortable darkness would wash over him, but that didn't seem to be in the cards for the young preacher. For whatever reason, he held on. The bird adjusted its position and made quick work of the priest's ankle, nabbing little bits of flesh, stealing away muscle from his calves, leaving everything from the knee down a patch-work of purple and red and bony-white.

It took Charlie a second to digest this, as it was all happening so fast—but once he did, he was able to get his gun up, close one eye, aim, and pull the trigger. The blast from this distance blew the bird away, leaving behind only a smattering of a few dozen feathers, the colors exotic, ranging from tropical greens to peacock blues and purples.

Charlie stood up and dusted the powdery, clingy sand off his knees.

That was when he heard Nellie shouting.

She was facing the sky.

It was filled with feathers and teeth.

"WHAT THE HELL IS THAT THING?" Nellie asked as she and Finn watched the bird divebomb and land dangerously close to Charlie without much warning. There was no use shouting to him; by the time the thing was in view, it had practically hit the ground.

As the bird executed its swift attack, pulling strands of meat away from the preacher's bones, Finn said, "Well, that's a *Nemicolopterus*. Nasty little fuckers. Eat you down to the bone like a pack of piranhas. Sky piranhas, that's what they call them."

"Who's them?" Nellie asked, wondering if she should give Charlie a hand. It was one small bird, and he had the drop on it, so she suspected he'd crown himself the victor in this fight. Still though—the ball of feathers and teeth seemed feisty enough to put up a decent struggle.

"Dinosaur buddies of mine."

"Dinosaur buddies?" She turned away from Charlie, who'd gone and blown the bird to bits, and faced Finn with an *oh-I-just-got-to-hear-this* look upon her face. "What the hell is that, exactly?"

"It's kinda sorta what it sounds. Friends and I get together, talk about dinosaurs. You know, learn stuff about them."

"You one of those obsessed types?"

"Not exactly. But dino watching is a hobby."

She thought there might be more to the story, something to come back to later. But she'd park the conversation for now, return when times became more appropriate. "I know what you did with that kid."

" 'Scuse me?"

"No way you rode out and back that quickly. Not unless you only made it halfway there and turned around, or unless you got some Indian magic tucked in that satchel of yours."

He didn't answer to that.

"Did you kill him?" she asked plainly, not that she'd beat around the bush anyway. She wasn't that type of girl, never had been.

"Didn't kill him. Did it like I said I did." Finn spit on the rock to his right, and Nellie turned to watch Charlie making sure the *Nemicolopterus* was good and dead. "Rode the boy into town and found him a caretaker."

"I don't believe you. Distance don't add up worth a shit. And I can spot a liar when I see one—Charlie can too, but he's much too polite to lob an accusation of this nature. He can spot a liar. A cheat. Suspect he's a good enough poker player, good enough to make it a serious side business when he's too old to chase around frontier vermin."

"The town was closer than—"

"Don't bullshit a bullshitter," she said. "That's something my pa used to say, something that always stuck." She felt her eyes go dark and cold for a second; hearing herself say the word *pa* pulled her away from the moment. She returned just as quickly, focusing in on the conversation at hand. "If I find out you killed that boy on account of...I don't know...sheer laziness? Pure sloth? I will gut you myself, and I'll make sure you're alive the entire time I'm pulling your 'testines out of that belly of yours."

"Jesus, lady. Gimme a break. I ain't the debased bastard you think I am."

Her eyes slimmed at him. "Bullshit a bullshitter."

Something flashed from above, and she screamed, an involuntary reaction to the sudden changing in the skies.

Finn unleashed his revolvers and started firing at the skyward attack. Feathery explosions popped like firecrackers. He shot one after another, and when Nellie uncovered her head from the initial wave of threats, she released her guns from their leathery corrals and started in on the killing. The small pterosaurs began to fill the sky, swooping in and going for their faces. The ones that managed to dodge the bullets and get through the traffic of exploded feathers and dislodged appendages reached their targets, extending their webbed claws with the hopes of scratching trenches into the humans' fleshy surfaces. It was a lot of ducking and diving for Finn and Nellie. And once they ran out of ammo, stopping to reload was a near impossibility; they needed to move and do so quickly, or the sky piranhas would shred them up easier than old, thin documents.

"Inside!" Nellie shouted, firing off her last round. It hit a descending bird directly in the face, and the decapitated body went flying into her right shoulder, splashing her forehead with a bloody-wet bolus of bird meat. Finn provided some cover, taking out a few birds, but mostly making enough noise to keep them at bay; they sure didn't like the guns when they talked, some of them taking back to the sky, returning to their circular patterns over the now-dead town.

Nellie reached the porch's overhang and immediately went to the front door, not bothering to look back and see what happened to Finn or if any birds were hot on her trail. Didn't matter to her, and the only thing that did was how fast she could get cover and pop some new rounds into her six-shooter. Once behind the door, she spun around, reaching for the ammo bag strapped to her hip. Finn was finishing up what was left in his chamber, and once the guns were spent, he sprinted toward cover. A few birds dove on top of him, pecking at his face, but he did a good enough job covering up and punching them away. He was able to get inside in a hurry, practically unscathed from the aerial assault.

"Fuckers," Nellie whispered, her guns fully stocked now.

Finn closed the door behind him.

Nellie moved along the exterior wall and over to the massive storefront window, gaining a glimpse of the outside world, the fury of feathers that had invaded the town's center. There was no sign of Charlie, which was either a really good thing or a really bad one, and she couldn't make up her mind which outcome swayed her.

Finn tapped her shoulder. "Um, Nellie."

"Not now," she said, trying to study the birds, their patterns, how they moved. She dreamt up scenarios of how they could escape this place. She also wondered if this storm of feathers and beaks would eventually pass like all storms eventually do.

"Look," Finn said, fiery.

She craned her head in the proposed direction, and in the back of the store, huddled behind a low counter containing jars stocked with hard candy, was about fifteen people, men, women, and children alike, all of them bathed in the blood of the dead, all of them wide-eyed and breathing heavily, looking at Finn and Nellie as if they were two devils gone and risen from the depths of the Great Lakes of Eternal Fire.

One of the men—perhaps the leader of this congregation, perhaps not—shoved an accusatory finger in their direction. Fear and general hatred expanded the whites of his eyes. "You brought the devils back down on us," he barked.

Finn and Nellie exchanged glances.

"When did they come?" Finn asked, turning back to the people. "The *Nemi*—the devils. How long ago?"

No one answered. Then a woman, her hair matted with dried blood and flecked with human gobbets, said, "Day before yesterday."

"You've holed up here for going on three days?" Nellie asked, astonished and not afraid to show so.

The group didn't answer, but their silence was answer enough. Nellie inspected the long, worn faces, the kids whose faces were crusty with days-old blood, clearly not theirs. In fact, most of the people seemed uninjured. One man held his arm in a way that suggested the bone there was broken. A few had garments wrapped around wounds that must have bled a lot. But that was it. No one had lost an eye or a limb. Just some flesh. The worst thing about the survivors were their eyes though, the torment swirling within them. The haunts that lived there now. It was all present, and Nellie's heart ached for them.

"They've come an' gone," a kid said, a small boy, and the look he earned from the grownups suggested they wished he'd kept quiet on the subject. "Few times. Every time one of us leaves, we don't come back."

"Joshua, hush," another woman said.

The man who'd accused them of devilry spoke again, though Nellie wished he hadn't. "And you brought them back. They'd gone away for a while, and now they're back again. We thought we were safe, and you—you sons of a bitches brought them back!"

"We didn't bring them from nowhere," Finn corrected. "They were here and never left, you brain-dead yokel."

"All right, enough is enough," Nellie said, stepping on Finn's toes—literally. She extended her right boot, and pressed her pointed toe down on Finn's, a subtle gesture to let him know he was making things much worse than they ought to be. "We're not gonna be stuck in here forever, that's for sure."

"Yeah? And how to do you know that, young missy?" The man seethed. "Those sky lizards done torn apart our town, killed nearly a hundred of us."

"Well, they probably know y'all are hiding in here and they're just waiting for you to donate more of your flesh." She shook your head. "You said you keep going out there? People keep leaving and not coming back?"

The man nodded. "We need to eat, dammit."

"Aye, you need to eat. So do they."

Finn cleared his throat. "How many guns y'all got?"

The man shrugged. "A few, I gather."

Finn rotated a finger in the air, circular patterns like the sky piranhas themselves. "These things didn't seem to like them. Most dinosaurs don't, even though *Pterosaurs* aren't technically dinosaurs, but..." She caught his eyes on her, and she threw a funny look his way. "I digress. Look, thing is—we could scare off these son-bitches if we got enough firepower. Give 'em a spook. They'll fly on."

"Son," the red-faced man said, leaning in. "You think we got enough bullets for every one of those birds up there?"

"No, certainly not. Low on ammo ourselves. But we stay low, shoot from the doors and windows, under cover, and they'll fly off. Swear on it."

The man looked to the others. No one offered to agree, but no one disagreed with Finn's idea either.

"Gather your guns, don't care if they shoot BBs or bullets.

Just go on and get them, whatever you got in this here establishment. Then meet back here in about ten minutes." Finn smiled, tipped his head, and then looked out the window. "We gonna have us bird for dinner."

CHARLIE MANAGED to escape the feathery onslaught and tucked himself into a shop adjacent to the one Finn and Nellie had run into. Ten minutes later the sky cleared, the heavens opening up a blue cloudless pasture. Not a bird in sight, though Charlie knew better. Or he *almost* knew better. The birds could have flown off in search of other towns to terrorize. But something about the way they cleared out made him doubt that was true. He had a feeling stepping one foot on the town's dirt drag would be like ringing the dinner bell before a wagon full of starved traveling folks.

So, he waited, spying across the street. He saw the horses were still hitched and wondered why the birds were only interested in humans, having left the horses untouched. It was probably an answer he wouldn't get, for like most animals, their intentions were secret. Regardless, the horses were still alive, and for that he was thankful. He hoped the birds wouldn't change their minds and come back to get something for their troubles.

In the window across the way, he saw waving. It was Nellie,

Finn next to her. She was waving and pointing to the door a few feet away. She wanted to talk was what he gathered from her actions. So, he moved away from his porthole and went to the door, pushing it open a crack, making sure not to push too hard. He didn't want the hinges shrieking loud enough to alert those deadly birds. When he did, he put an ear to the gap and listened.

"We're gonna make a stand, Charlie!" Nellie shouted across the street.

A stand? Had she seen the same attack he had? Been in it? He knew she had but—whew! What exactly were they supposed to stand with? There were hundreds of those flying predators, possibly a thousand, and he had (maybe) fifty rounds on him.

"Y'all lose your minds or something?" Charlie called back.

"We have more guns! Survivors in here!"

Charlie sighed. *Survivors?* Interesting. He wondered how many, but figured it wasn't important. The important thing was he trusted Nellie, and she wouldn't confront this horde of villainous sky rats if she didn't think they could take them.

"All right. What's the plan?"

"The plan..." she said, stepping out onto the porch, leaving the safety of the building behind her. Finn was in tow, and slowly, more figures materialized from the shadows within. At least six more gunslingers, average townsfolk who probably knew some basics but weren't worth much of a shot. He'd been wrong about such things before, but not often. "The plan, Charlie Archer, is to aim, shoot, and kill, and do little thinking about anything else."

She raised her gun and fired at the sky.

The first bird dropped like piss in a bucket.

FINN CONNECTED with his first six shots—six bullets, six birds. They fell to the earth like clothes at the end of a hard workday. Feathers burst apart, shooting in all directions, a pillow fight fought by invisible folks. He kept shooting, taking out the bastards as they came, and when he needed to reload, there were three other guns ready to provide cover. They worked like this in tandem, much like the three of them had done back in Oat Creek saving the town from the *Tyrannosaurs*.

This was different because there were more threats, and the threats came from the skies and the targets were smaller. If they didn't have the added guns of the survivors, they wouldn't have stood a chance. But the extra firepower proved to be the difference maker, and after about ten minutes of battling the birds, the numbers sailing above them had dwindled to a countable tally. The ones left remained in the sky, high enough so that any shot from the ground would be a praying man's gamble, and not one of the shooters were dumb enough to waste a bullet on such an attempt. The birds seemed to know exactly where that threshold was and held to it. And soon after, when the dust had settled and the gun-smoke cleared, leaving behind a hazy glow to the small town that smelled like some cavernous dead world, the birds left the sky altogether and sailed on.

There were no long thank-yous or goodbyes. There were hardly any words at all. A few nods, a couple handshakes. After that, Charlie told the man who'd alleged that Finn and Nellie were devils and brought along the devil's business that he wished the trio could stay behind, help clear the dead, cook the birds and feast on their kills, but they had to move on.

"Other business is calling," he told him, but the man didn't reply, not with his mouth. His eyes thanked him, thanked *all* of them, but he never did apologize for calling them devils.

That was okay with Finn.

In a lot of ways, he felt like one.

A devil in human flesh.

3

FEATHERS IN THE JUNGLE * THEY CAME FOR BLOOD *
TRUTHS * CABIN BY THE LAKE * COLD ALES AND OLD,
LONG TALES * FRANCIS DRAWS AN ACE

Charlie couldn't remember the last time he'd crossed the state line into Wyoming, but the last time he had, he sure hadn't seen lush jungles and open green valleys. A lot had changed since his last adventure to this particular territory, and this vast slice of land didn't exactly remind him of the traditional American West. But...things change. People do, too. And sometimes landscapes. Although, he thought both transformations were more of the gradual sort. In any case, the map he'd kept took them through the western jungles, past lakes and rivers and treacherous terrain he hoped the horses would handle with ease.

He kept an eye on Finn. Although he had pulled his weight on the trail, helping with directions and hunting for rabbits and indigenous turkeys, Charlie didn't trust him one hundred percent. He had a quality that filled Charlie with some unease, and he didn't like the arithmetic regarding the ride back to that town where he supposedly delivered Willy McClellan. But...he had no proof that he'd done anything *but* what had been agreed upon. Still...there was the doubt, and the doubt ate away at him like fleas on their blood-bag host.

They moved into thicker areas of the forest where the trail grew thinner and the branches scraped the sides of their horses and the foliage needed to be moved by their own hands to prevent their faces from being carved. Mosquitos were a chief annoyance, buzzing and biting, drawing feasts of blood from them. Finn must have had some allergy to their saliva because his neck swelled with red bumps.

"You okay?" Charlie asked him, motioning to the bites.

"Yeah, damn mosquitos." He scratched at another one. "Happens all the time. I'll get over it. Find some chickweed and you let me know."

"Don't know that I'd recognize chickweed if I saw it, but I'll do my best. Maybe Nellie can—"

Nellie stopped her horse with a sudden jerk of the reins. Charlie thought (for a split second) that it was because he had mentioned her name and doing so had somewhat alarmed her, but that was a dumb way of thinking. No, something else had grabbed her attention, and since she was in the lead, they all stopped. The horses let out some defiant neighs, but not one of them bucked, which Charlie considered a blessing. Horses tended to spook easier in forests than out in the open. Less visibility seemed to put every living creature on edge, and the horses were sometimes worse than barn cats when it came to getting scared. Charlie himself could feel his heart rate climbing, so he wouldn't blame the geldings if their front hooves lifted from the soil.

"What is it?" Charlie whispered.

Nellie shushed him and put her ear to the wind. Listened. Went on listening for a good thirty seconds, and just before Charlie was about to re-ask his initial query, she said, "Something is hunting us."

Charlie swallowed, and then scanned the trees. He didn't see any evidence of a hunt, but that didn't mean squat as far as Charlie Archer was concerned. He'd been snuck up on by pack-hunting dinosaurs before. Wouldn't be the first time, and if he continued to bounty hunt, journeying across the American frontier, then it probably wouldn't be the last time either. He just didn't know how many times he could keep surviving them. Some species had the art of the hunt down to a science. *Raptors*, mostly.

"Well, shit—that's a problem," Charlie said, and he meant it. Checking his pouch on the side of the saddle, seeing what was left of the ammunitions, he said, "Those birds back there used up a lot of my supply, and I don't suppose there's an ammo shop out here in the jungle."

"Will you shut up?" she more or less yelled, but her voice was low, a whisper, designed to get her point across and not attract the attention of their pursuers.

"*Velociraptors*?" Finn asked, keeping his voice as low as he could.

Nellie shook her head. "Bigger."

Charlie inhaled a sharp breath. "How many?"

"I see one," she replied, "but that means at least six."

"Which species?"

Nellie nodded in the direction of whatever she saw as she slowly went for the gun on her hip.

Charlie inspected the referenced area, and it took a moment for his mind to see what she saw. Through the foliage, about a solid thirty feet away, he saw a single eye, yellow, surrounded by dark feathers that seemed to fit in perfectly with the leafy shadows the jungle provided. He could almost make out the red feathery crest atop the predator's head.

"I see it," Finn said. His voice wavered, and his trembling hand went for his six-shooter. "*Utahraptor.*"

"Shit," Charlie said. "Think they followed us through Utah?"

"Hard to believe that. No, we would have spotted them. Or they would have attacked us when we made camp. No, they have a nest up here somewhere. I'd bet my bottom dollar on it."

"Will you two shut *the fuck* up!" Nellie snapped. "Jesus Lord, have mercy."

Charlie did finally listen. For a few seconds, at least. After he got out his gun and made sure he was fully loaded, he grabbed the reins in case a race was about to start. *Utahraptors* were much larger than *Velociraptors* and their nasty cousins, the *Deinonychus,* and that meant they couldn't run as fast. A horse could easily beat them in a sprint, but that would have to mean an open field or the flat desert. *Utahraptors* were still limber enough to navigate the twists and turns a forest trail might provide, and that meant they were in danger, especially if the hunters had them boxed in, which was exactly what Nellie had suggested.

"We running?" Charlie said. "Or are we dancing?"

Nellie turned her head. "We're running."

"All right," Charlie said, putting the gun away. The others did the same. "On the count of three?"

"One...two...three," Nellie said quietly, and then dug her spurs into her mare's ribs.

THE HORSES TOOK off like a speeding bullet at a sundown showdown. They were able to take the *Utahraptors* by surprise and get ahead of the one that Nellie had spotted. And thank the Good Lord she had because if she hadn't, they would have walked their horses right into the trap. That was the thing about the West—you always had to keep your peepers open and your mind engaged. One miscalculation or wrong step could mean certain death. And Nellie had managed to help them avoid that particular scenario on this day.

Charlie would thank her later when they were safe. For now, he concentrated on the trail, getting his gelding to take the turns as if he were barrel racing, sharp cuts that led into another straightaway flanked by towering leafy oaks with trunks the width of whiskey barrels. Snarling and chirping followed their every move, and Charlie afforded himself a glance over his shoulder when he thought their lead was lengthening. He was sad to discover that the distance between them and the pack wasn't all that much, and that he could actually smell their dirty-bird stink when he tilted his head to the side. The leader seemed to grow quite angry with him when he stole that brief glance—the *Utahraptor's* jaws opened wide, exposing its long pink tongue. The red crest atop its black-feathered head flopped along with the tremendous strides it took at its top speed. Charlie glanced down at the dewclaws on both feet and suddenly recalled watching one of them rip through a man's belly with the graceful ease of a hot blade through a sponge cake.

Charlie thought they were gaining on them, and since he brought up the tow, it was his duty to do something about it. He freed his Colt and aimed for the pack leader, right at that feathery dome. Pulled the trigger. With his horse topping out at max speed, the ride was a little bumpy and his aim was slightly off. The shot wasn't wasted, though—it sailed past the pack leader and into one of its followers, skinning the animal's snout and causing it to veer from its direct path. It didn't put the bull down as he'd hoped, but it slowed him some. There were still four more giving chase and Charlie didn't want to waste all the bullets he had left. Maybe one more.

He aimed again, waited this time, trying to compensate for the horse's breakneck speed, the jouncing. When he thought he had the rhythm down, he tugged the trigger, listened to the .45's sweet thunder, and watched a bloody firework blossom behind the pack leader's head. The dinosaur went down immediately, and, as luck would have it, took out the other *Utahraptors* as it went crashing into them. One of them managed to avoid the disaster, leaping over the tumbling mess of feathers and bared teeth, but by the time it reached top speed, Charlie and the gang had already put ample distance between them. Took another quarter mile, but the *Utahraptor* abandoned his lonely pursuit. The beasts had come for blood, but they left with clean teeth.

Charlie could breathe again.

They all could.

They rode on.

THERE WAS a way station farther on up ahead, and since they thought the pack of *Utahraptors* could no longer smell them or catch up in any way, they stopped to catch their breaths, water their horses, and break bread. Nellie was still on edge. She drank from the well the way station provided, and then put some water in a bucket for her horse, Sunshine, to lap from. After, she gave Sunshine some grain and then let her graze on the grass around the outskirts, along with the two other horses. She kept an eye on her, though—the run-in with the *Utahraptors* had left her on edge, and she could never be certain that they wouldn't follow them this far. Or...that more dangers weren't lurking in these Wyoming forests.

The way station sat atop a small hill, flat enough to build such a structure. The forests surrounded them on almost every side, mountainous hills rose all around them. Birdsong filled the air. Butterflies danced from dandelion to dandelion in the surrounding, verdant grasslands. The wind was crisp up here, and even though they were high up, Nellie found it easier to breathe. Something about being elevated refreshed her bones and relieved her spine from the encroaching saddle pain she often got from a long ride.

Once their bellies were full and the horses were rested (with full bellies of their own), they hitched their rides to the station's post and headed inside to talk to the station keeper. A lone man sat inside at the welcome table, a mug of coffee in one hand, a newspaper in the other. Scruffy red fuzz covered the lower half of his face, the untamed beard growth hiding the man's neck. A tame and gentle blue filled out his eyes. He chewed his tobacco and spat long muddy-brown streams into the bucket near his feet. Once he saw he had guests, he put the paper down and the coffee mug too.

"Well, howdy strangers," he said. "Been riding long? Y'all look some kind of whipped."

"It's been a rough outing," Charlie said with an amiable smile.

The man looked at him, his eyes growing with uncomfortable suspicion. "If y'all are planning a robbery, I hate to inform you that no money is kept at this here way station."

Charlie let out a brief chuckle. "No, no. Never planned a robbery in my entire life, and I ain't starting now." He sighed and took up the chair across from the man, seating himself without waiting for an invitation. "Just the opposite, actually. We are sort of on the other side of the law."

"Sort of."

"Bounty hunter folk."

"Ah," the man said, as if this were a refreshment. "I understand. Well, thank you for your service. Bounty hunters do a lot of dirty work these days, and I don't think folks appreciate them all that much."

"It's just a job," Charlie assured him. "We do what we can."

"Name's Nutley," he said, extending a handshake Charlie's way. Charlie shook his hand. And then so did Finn. Nellie was last. "I know who *you* are, little lady," he said before Nellie had the opportunity to introduce herself. "Yeah, I seen you in a gunfight tournament out near Albuquerque. Oh, man. You really showed them boys what was what, I tell you."

Charlie smiled, hints of a soft chuckle bleeding through. "Looks like you got a new fan, Nellie Watts."

"Oh, I bet she's got many fans." Nutley's belly trembled as a laugh rose up and out his mouth. "You're faster and more accurate than anyone I've ever seen before."

"I appreciate your words, mister," she said sheepishly. "But we don't have a lot of time and we need a place to rest before we head back out. Important work awaits us."

Nutley gave her a two-fingered salute. "Yes, ma'am. Happy to help anyway I can. Got some cots in the back there—help yourselves to them. Changed the sheets just yesterday and I haven't had any visitors in about a week."

"Not many folks come up this way?" Finn asked, examining the dull walls, the paintings that were mounted every five feet or so. Photos of cowboys and landscapes. Stuff Nellie could find in just about any general store and for cheap.

"Not too many," Nutley said. "Not too many at all."

"What about the wildlife?" Charlie said. "Our horses safe for the night?"

"Aye. Safe. Haven't had an incident in the two years I've been here."

"How long do you stay?" Finn asked.

At this, Nutley gave him a queer look. "Asking a lot of questions there." A gruff laugh escaped him; whether he meant to or not, Nellie could not decipher. "Didn't realize I was going to be interrogated by a bunch of bounty hunters."

No one talked Nutley down from whatever hill he was climbing.

"All right," he said, realizing that Finn was asking a serious question and was expecting a serious answer. "Two weeks. We rotate, me and my partner."

"What's your partner's name?"

This earned him a dirty look, and Nutley's eyes lingered on Finn. Nellie thought the look meant he wished to strangle him. This wasn't the way to make friends, and she wondered why

Finn was pressing the man so persistently. She also wondered why Charlie, unspoken leader of their trio, hadn't requested that Finn stuff a cork in it.

"Uh...Billy," Nutley said.

"Billy what? Billy got a last name, Mr. Nutley?"

"Now, come on—what kind of ham is this?"

Charlie finally turned to Finn. "Why don't you ease up on the man, Finn? He's been nothing but courteous to us."

"Last name," Finn pressed. "Billy's."

Nutley's lips stiffened as a dark ruddy color bloomed on his cheeks. "Billy Winthrope."

"Where's your horse?"

"Excuse me?" Anger now. No evidence of anything but.

"Your horse. Surely you have one. Didn't see her outside."

"All right," Nutley said, pushing himself up from the table. "That's enough. I don't have to listen to—"

Finn drew his weapon and pointed it at the center of Nutley's broad chest. "You move another muscle, I'll blow a hole through you and that's a goddamn promise, friend."

"We ain't friends, stranger," Nutley hissed. "And put that damn gun down before you do something you gonna regret for the rest of your days, something you gon' end up apologizing for when God calls you home."

"Don't talk to me about God," Finn said. *"Murderer."*

"Murderer?" the man asked, a smile appearing in all that red fuzz. "Murderer? Sir, have you gon' and lost your goddamn mind?"

"Nope, I haven't."

Charlie cleared his throat. "Finn, I suggest you calm down and explain these accusations in a manner we can all under-stand. You know, bring clarity to the sort."

Finn took a minute to look over the man, examine his face, his eyes going soft during the inspection. Then, a slick, knowing smile captured his lips. "Worked as a station keeper going back a few years ago. Wasn't there long, not more than a few months, just something to do and pass the time, earn me a couple bits before I looked for something better. During that time, I got pretty friendly with how things were run by the Pioneer company. This is a Pioneer station, ain't it?"

Nutley didn't speak. He just continued to glare at Finn as if he was indeed a murderer, and Finn was aiming to be his next victim.

"Yeah, that's what I thought."

"What's this amount to, Finn?" Charlie asked. "Dying to know."

"Well, Charlie," Finn said, stepping closer, ensuring a clean shot should he need to pull the trigger. Jury was out on that possibility, but Nellie didn't have a good feeling about any of this. She longed for a sense of normalcy. Couldn't they make one stop without putting their lives in jeopardy?

Such is the way of the west, darlin', her daddy's phantom voice spoke in her mind. *Such is the way.*

Hearing that replay brought a sting to her eyes.

"Pioneer companies make their keepers work three-week shifts, not two. And..." He nodded at Nutley and then used his gun-less hand to grab the five-day scruff on his own chin. "They require a clean face. Smooth like a baby's bottom. Ain't that right...Nutley? It is Nutley, isn't it? Or is that name just as phony as the pretenses that you've presented?"

There was no backlash, not at first. Then, the man's lips spread. "He's lying," Nutley said with little emotion.

"Am not." He pointed a finger at him as if his hand itself was a gun ready to fire. "You are. And I figured something was amiss when I found that patch of grass soaked in fresh blood."

"Blood?" Charlie said, turning full toward him. "Why didn't you tell us?"

"Didn't know what to make of it, really," Finn told him. "Thought it could have been an animal or a dinosaur, something that got hurt. But...that didn't add up."

"What are you saying?" Nellie asked. "That Nutley here killed someone? A man who'd been here before us?"

"Yep, that's what I'm saying. I'm saying that this lying sack of shit ain't no keeper for the Pioneer company, and furthermore, he murdered the man who'd been here only an hour before."

The accusation lingered in the air. Everyone digested the information at their own pace, but Charlie was the first one to respond.

"What say you, Nutley?" he asked.

"He's lying. That's all there is to it."

"You got red on you," Finn said, pointing to his shirt. Up near the collar, there was indeed a dark, drying splotch of red staining the fabric. "You might have washed yourself better. Probably would have helped your case there...*friend*."

There was another bout of silence, and then Nutley hung his head in surrender. No one else challenged him. To Nellie, it looked like the truth was spoken in that moment. That lingering quiet was admission enough.

Nutley went for his mug of hot coffee, the one he'd undoubtedly stolen, grabbed the handle and flung the contents in Finn's direction. Then he took off for the closest window, not that he could fit through any one of them. But he tried anyway, speeding forth, lowering his shoulder, preparing to meet the glass. Finn sidestepped the airborne mug quite easily, dodging the hot, steaming contents hurling forth. Then he went and put two bullets in the guilty party: one in his back, one in his neck. His stubby hands went to the bright scarlet hole near his throat as his legs gave out, causing him to fall to the dusty floorboards.

Finn made his way around the desk, keeping the gun trained on him, and Nellie expected him to put one last hole in him, this one between the eyes. But he didn't. Not yet. He waited, watched as the man, whose true name may or may not have been Nutley, squirmed in pain and flipped over onto his back. Blood poured through the cracks in his fingers. Gasping for clean air, his face tightened, teeth chattered, and the extra weight in his cheeks trembled.

"You got anything to say for yourself, you sorry son of a bitch," Finn asked, the second his shadow fell over him.

The man spat on his boots.

"That's what I thought." Cocking back the hammer, he prepared to end him.

"Wait a second," Charlie said, creeping up behind Finn, placing a hand on the gun and lowering it some. "No sense in killing him."

"And why's that?" Finn asked, seeming not exactly astonished—sort of as if he was expecting it.

"Because...even though the evidence is overwhelming," Charlie said, "we don't have a body and we ain't the law. We should leave him tied up and report what we've found to a local sheriff. Let them handle things."

"What if he escapes?" Finn asked.

Nellie watched the man's brow bubble with sweat.

"You can't execute a defenseless man," Charlie said plainly. "You don't have that right, Finn Hampton. None of us do."

Still, he didn't remove the gun from its potential target. "We could leave him outside. Maybe those raptors get him. Wouldn't be our fault. Let nature bring on the justice."

"Leaving him to die is the same as pulling that there trigger, and you know that." Charlie lowered the gun even more, and Finn allowed it to fall. Once the barrel was aimed at the ground and presented no more of a threat to the man allegedly named Nutley, Finn took off in the opposite direction. "Good choice," Charlie said, seeing him off.

Finn went for the door, pushed open the barrier, and stepped out into the sunshine.

Charlie glanced over at Nellie, and Nellie simply said, "I'll talk to him."

Charlie nodded, and said, "I'll get the rope and tie up Nutley here."

OUTSIDE, she found Finn pacing, working off his anger. Sipping a glass of water, she watched him go through the motions, imagining the thoughts skipping through his head.

"You all right, kid?" she asked. *Kid,* she thought. He was probably only a few years younger than she. "You went all freaky on us back there. Saw the light in your eyes dim. Something dark come over them."

"I'm fine."

"Don't look it."

"That man killed another man and he deserved to die."

"Well, hard to argue that." She eyed him cautiously. "You got a dark streak to you, Finn Hampton. Not sure I like it."

He looked out across the hill, past the greens and into the dark shadows of the forests around them.

"How'd you know?" she asked.

He turned to her. "Told you—worked for the Pioneer—"

"You never worked for the Pioneer company, Finn, and don't pretend like you did."

The color drained from his face. A shade of embarrassment flushed his cheeks. For a second, she thought he might pull his weapon on her, start shooting. But she knew he wouldn't dare—she'd beat him to the trigger faster than he could blink.

"No," he admitted. "No, I never did."

"Then how'd you know?"

He nodded, revealing he had no choice but to speak the truth. "What was it you said to me a few days back? 'Don't bullshit a bullshitter?'"

She glared on.

"Yeah," he said, pushing his tongue against his inner cheek. "Yeah, that was it. All it was."

She didn't ask another thing. Instead, she watched him walk out into the field, allowing him to bask in the green warmth and the fresh breaths the mountain air provided.

THEY STAYED THE NIGHT, each taking two hour shifts to watch the tied-up Nutley just in case he did indeed somehow break free. But he didn't, and they got through the night. Come morning, they fed the man and gave him enough water to get him through the next day or two, and then set off in search of the nearest town.

They found one about two hours north, told the local lawmen what had transpired up at the way station on the mountain trail, and then left that town in search of their true purpose—to find the outlaw Francis Burner and his mischievous crew of criminals.

Along the way, they stopped to watch a herd of herbivores dine on the vegetation in a low valley somewhere in the south-west region of Wyoming. As Finn watched the herd with the fascination a six-year-old boy might, Charlie checked his map, and the folded piece of paper, yellowed and worn thin by time, told them they were getting closer to their destination. Another three days or so and they'd arrive at *Pteranodon* Canyon.

"So peaceful out here," Finn told them, grinning at the herd of *Stegosauruses* as they fed upon the green meadows. "When I was a boy, my pa used to take me down to Cedar Crow Valley—a small valley in the heart of Mississippi—and watch the *Triceratops* herds migrate north. It was so peaceful watching them."

Charlie committed the next portion of their ride to memory, and then rolled up the map, tucking it back into his saddle bag. "Yeah, kid. Some of them are damn peaceful. And some of them ain't."

"Don't I know it."

He went quiet in that moment, and Charlie wondered where his mind had run off to. He didn't want to ask, for such places in the mind were private territories, but he didn't want to go on ignoring the torment that had been very clearly etched into his features. If Charlie was being honest, he'd noticed a change in Finn since they had departed the way station. It was as if his mind was in constant war with itself.

"My father was eaten by a *Tyrannosaur*. Happened when I was eight years old, at the ranch he owned. My mother, brother, and I were able to escape—got back into the house. My father, he'd seen them coming. A bull and a cow, much like the ones we tangoed with back in Oat Creek. They got him, though. He was smart enough to run away from the house, lead them away far enough so they didn't return. I got upstairs and was able to see the whole thing—how they tracked him down, how they hunted him. He did a good job trying to outsmart them, throwing rocks and distracting them, running in the opposite direction, ducking behind trees—but in the end, it didn't matter. They tracked him down, and I watched my pa meet their teeth."

"Sorry to hear about that, Finn. Had no idea." It was the best Charlie could respond with.

"Have nightmares about them sometimes. The *Tyrannosaurs*. They come for me at night. Tear me apart. Just like they did my daddy."

"Horrible."

"I've heard you murmuring in your sleep," Nellie said, taking up the grassy seat next to him. "Heard you crying. Whimpering something awful."

Finn sniffled as if he might be crying now. "They're terrible dreams."

"I can imagine, the way you carry on in your sleep."

Charlie had never heard Finn make a peep, but that was because Charlie slept like the dead. Plus, if Finn had cried a tear in his dreams, it was of no concern to him. A man's dreams were his problems to deal with, and his alone.

"I have bad dreams too," Nellie admitted. "My father's still alive but just barely. Might as well be dead; hasn't left his bed in years. But he's still kicking, that fiery old soul. See, he's got a sickness buried in him, something eating him from the inside out, and local doctors back in Kansas don't have any answers. Just told me to wise up and accept that he won't be around much longer. And maybe that's true. But they have these doctors in New York who specialize in these types of things, and well, as you can imagine their type of practices cost a shiny penny. So... that's why I was eager to jump on this trip. The purse will be enough to transport my father to New York, get him looked at by some of the finest doctors this country has to offer."

The men stood silent for a minute. Charlie was unsure how to proceed from this truth.

Then, Finn said, "I didn't kill that boy."

Stunned, Charlie made his way over and kneeled down in front of the man. "You have something to say you better say it. Right here and now, before we go any further."

Tears stood on the brims of Finn's eyes, threatening to fall. He avoided Charlie's stern gaze, continuing to look down upon the valley, the peaceful congregation of *Stegosauruses*. "I didn't kill him, but I know that's what the two of you think. I made it back because...I left him in that town. I didn't knock on no doors, didn't find him safe house to hold up in, didn't find him a caretaker."

"You lyin' son of a bitch," Charlie said through his teeth. "You said that you handed him off to a caretaker, that someone agreed to take him in."

"I didn't want to lose a day riding with y'all, and the town— it's a good town, I know it—and I knew someone would take him in once they found him."

Charlie grabbed him by the collar, shaking him like he would a coconut tree. "You dropped him off in the middle of the night. He could have wandered!"

"He was fine!" Finn shouted back, tears pouring out of him now, his face slick with a crystal sheen. "Honest! He was fine! He wasn't going anywhere! I made sure of it!"

Charlie shook the man again, with more force this time. He waited for Nellie to intervene, considering she and Finn clearly had something going on—a platonic something, something far from romantic, but something all the same. A sibling-like connection, perhaps. Born from the same womb called misery. "How? How did you *make sure* of it?"

Finn's eyes rolled, and Charlie learned he was choking him too hard. He eased up some. *Some,* but not all the way.

"I...I tied him to a hitching post. Tied a good knot. There was no loosening it. Made sure!"

Charlie seemed satisfied by this, not that he enjoyed being previously lied to, nor did he like the fact that Finn didn't follow through on their original agreement. Letting go, he stepped back, unable to break his vision from the groveling Finn Hampton.

"Please...forgive me. It was...it was dumb, I see that now. I shouldn't have left him. I shouldn't have."

Charlie looked to Nellie, who only shrugged as her eyebrows rose and fell in quick succession. "Get up," he told the man, and Finn sprung to his feet like the ground were a bed of hot coals. "I don't like being lied to, Finn Hampton. Hope you recognize that going forward. I don't see us having much use for each other after *Pteranodon* Canyon, but until then, I'd appreciate it if you kept your lies to a minimum. Or...keep them to none at all."

"I'm sorry. So sorry. It won't...won't happen again."

"See that it doesn't," Charlie said and left it at that.

The *Stegosauruses* continued to graze, but Charlie didn't stay to watch them. Instead, he prepared their camp and spent the rest of the day studying his map, the path toward the inevitable end, and he thought of how good it would feel to close his hands around the throat of one Francis Burner, squeeze those airways shut until every drop of life leaked from his cold, murderous eyes.

A FEW CLICKS north of the *Stegosaurus* herd on the following bright, blinding morning, Nellie said, "I know a place we can stop and stock up on supplies. Running low on canned foods and bullets." Those were two things they'd need to get through the days ahead—canned food was always a plus for the trail life. Made hunting less of a necessity and ensured they wouldn't go to bed with empty, angry bellies. The bullets—well, she figured there were more dangers out there, and was surprised they hadn't run into more along the way. They hadn't even seen a super predator since that initial run-in with the *Tyrannosaurs* back at Oat Creek. Not that she was complaining—it was a nice break from the norm. Traveling life was easily fifty percent trying to outrun things that could kill you, and they had been damn lucky not to stumble across a *rex* nest, or one of their cousins—an *Allosaur* or hell, even one of those *Giganotosaurs*. The latter being much taller that the *T. rex* and often more aggressive. She'd had a run-in with a bull a few years back. Ended up hiding down in an abandoned bear cave and waiting it out. Two days she spent in there just to be sure the thing wasn't coming back. She remembered having to rub wet mud all over her body to mask her smell. Worked though. She was able to journey back to the nearest town and all was well that ended well. But she would never forget those two moons she spent in that dark cave, praying that a smaller dinosaur wouldn't come finish what the giant carnivore could not.

Damn lucky and she knew it.

"Where's that?" Charlie asked, taking on the leadership role that was always suspected but never verbally agreed upon. He'd been that way the past few days, and it had become obvious when he confronted Finn about how he handled the transport of Willy McClellan.

"Just up yonder, a couple clicks," she told him.

"This town got a name?"

"No name. Not a town. It's a beautiful, idyllic cabin near the lake."

"Sounds peaceful," Charlie said. "And this cabin, it belongs to someone you know?"

"Sure does. Old friend."

"Boyfriend? Husband?"

She smiled. "Friend."

And it was left at that.

She led them off Charlie's mapped path but not too far, and eventually they ended up at the aforementioned cabin by the lake, though it was a bit farther than previously projected. Charlie didn't seem to mind, and if he did, he spoke nothing of the added distance.

"Here we are," she said, gazing upon the cabin by the lake. It didn't seem like much from the outside, and inside probably wasn't the cozy space you'd get from most rentals, but it was something, and right about now Nellie Watts could use a friendly face and a hot, decent meal.

"Who owns it?" Finn asked.

"Name's Barney Reeves." She dismounted her horse and tied her to a tree at the edge of the property.

The men followed her lead.

Then, the three marched up the small incline, toward the cabin by the lake. Stars were beginning to bleed through the sky, dusk settling in on the horizon. As they reached the porch, a gray-bearded Black man armed with a twelve-gauge opened up the front door. He didn't aim the weapon at his guests, more-or-less holding it for comfort. The two men stood back, but Nellie didn't miss a beat.

"Come on now, Barn," she said to him, her face glowing. "You really going to greet Nellie Watts with that ol' peashooter you got there?"

"Peashooter! *Paw!* This gun right here will blow a hole in you so wide I could serve a hamburger through you, like the window in a traveling food cart. A window! That's right, this gun right here could blow a window through you, girl." A deepening smile pushed his cheeks apart. "Well hell, look what the ghosts dragged in!" He leaned back into the cabin and shouted, "Martina! We got ourselves company!"

"Martina in there?" Nellie asked. "Oh, good. I getta two-for-one-er!" She conquered the stairs with one giant leap. Wrapping her hands around the old cowboy, she said, "I missed you, Barn, shit I've missed you a lot."

"Well hell, girl, I missed you too. Only been two years since you come an' visit me. The hell took you so long?"

She stared at him gravely, the happiness from a second ago dancing from her eyes.

"Well hell..." Barney said, with way less enthusiasm than he'd previously let on. "Why don't you come on in and tell ol' Barney all about it, huh?" He stepped aside so she could enter freely, and then turned to the other two men, who hadn't taken the stairs yet. As if they weren't sure the hospitable welcome was meant for them too. "Well, come on you two. Friends of Nellie's are friends of ol' Barney's. Pleasure to meet you boys." He flashed him the warmest smile he could, given Nellie's demeanor, then followed with, "Don't mind the shooter. I carry it everywhere I goes."

Charlie was the first to step forward. He tipped his hat to the cowboy. "Pleasure is mine, Barney. We've been riding hard and fierce, and you're one of the few friendly faces we've come across. Can't thank you enough."

"Well hell, don't thank me yet." There was a twinkle in his eyes, one that not even Nellie could decode. "I haven't agreed to nothin' yet."

This came with a hearty laugh.

"Haw, haw," Barney said. "Just kidding, y'all. Come inside. Sit down. Take a load off. We got ales. Cold ones too!"

"How'd you get them so cold?" Finn asked after swallowing the best ale he'd ever put his lips on.

"Well hell, that's the secret, isn't it?" Barney laughed. "Guess I can tell you. It's not that big of a secret and I'm sure you could figure it out, if you thought on it a minute."

Martina brought them all another round, almost as cold as the first. She kissed her husband atop his thinning head of curly white hair, and then took up the seat next to him. She was an accommodating host, and Finn wondered how people could grow so nice and hospitable in violent times like these. They weren't paying for bed and board—least not that he was aware of—and this treatment went far above what he'd received in most of those places.

"It's all about the lake," Barney Reeves stated, flicking a

finger toward the window that looked out across the lake. The
moon was out now, and Finn could see the broken white reflection of the luminous sky-rock on the black water's surface. "That
lake's good this time of year for keeping things nice and cool.
Even in the hot months it keeps things on the chilly side. I brew
the ales myself, bottle them, then put them in those." He
pointed to a couple of contraptions resting in the corner of the
room. To Finn, they looked like lobster cages, the kind he'd seen
back east when he had lived a year in Rhode Island in a small
village on the coast. "They're weighted and they sit on the
bottom, right in the coldest part of the lake."

"That's mighty impressive," Charlie told him. "Hard to find
cool beers in the summer months."

"Well, it sure beats harvesting ice from the mountains and
storing it in the cellar." Barney took another sip from his beer,
licking his lips and letting go of a refreshed sigh. "Pretty good
brew if I do say so myself."

Finn looked over at Nellie, who'd grown distant from their
talk of cool ales. "How'd you two meet anyway?" Curiosity had
bested him. She shot him a look that was almost pleading, a *do-
we-have-to-approach-that-subject,* but then Finn thought if there
were some secret behind them knowing each other, she probably wouldn't have brought them here in the first place. Still, *old
friends* wasn't enough to satisfy Finn's sometimes uncontrollable
quest for knowing all things.

Nellie sighed deeply, as if the subject was one of internal
contention. "Barney Reeves and my father were friends."

"Well hell, girl, don't undersell it. We was best friends, we
were. Best of friends. We went everywhere and did everything
together. We never went a day without talking to each other.
He's a great man, your father. Great man. Gave me my first job as
a free man, he did. When I got my freedom papers in sixty-three,
he brought me on as a deputy in Polk City. Next eight years, we

spent cleaning up that town, taking it back from the swine and swindlers who was stealing from those townspeople. Remember that, girl?"

"I remember," Nellie said with some fondness. Not too much, but some.

"Well hell, you were already starting to go off near the end of those eight years, taking to the road. He never could keep you down. You were always trying escape Polk City, weren't you?"

"Suppose I was."

"Man, we had some good times. But...all good things come to an end, don't they?"

"Well...what happened?" Finn asked.

"What happened?" Barney asked, shooting Finn a look that suggested the young gunslinger had fallen off his rocker. "What happened? Son, look at me. I became an old man is what happened. I was already fifty-one when I got my papers in sixty-three. Now I'm sixty-two and retired two years already."

"Sorry," Finn said, thinking he might have insulted the man. He couldn't tell. Barney's face was oddly animated, the way a traveling stage actor might portray certain emotions. He could have been truly insulted by Finn's question...or not. Either way, Finn would have believed it. "Didn't mean it like that."

"Well hell, that's okay, son. Ten years doesn't make a lot of difference when youse young like yourself—but when youse older—ah hellfire, ten years can feel like putting yourself through a meat grinder." At this, he swung his head in Nellie's direction. "So come out with it. What's this visit all about?"

Nellie hung her head.

"Come on," Barney said, taking a deep breath. "I know you didn't come on out here just to check up on ol' Barney Reeves. Figure there's an alternative reason behind you showing up and all. Not that I don't appreciate the company. Things can get lonely with just Martina and myself. No offense, Martina baby, I love you."

Martina, as quiet as she had been, didn't speak a word, but she didn't seem offended in the least.

"Dad's sick," Nellie said, her face losing some of its color. She took a long sip of her ale, finishing about quarter of the glass in one sip. "He's dying."

"Well hell," Barney said, his eyes softening. "Damn shame. Good man, that Sylvester Watts. Good man indeed, best I've ever known. But he an old man. Surprised the tough bastard's hung on this long, considering all and what we've been through. Shit, girl—what's he got?"

"Ain't a name for it yet."

"Ah, the nameless kind of disease. Nameless diseases be of the devil's work, of that I'm certain." Barney nodded as if he was taking in the information, processing it. The silence ended after he finished off the remainder of his beer. "Well, that all you come for? To tell me the old man was dying? Ruining my evening with this information? Tell you the truth, I thought that the second you gone and showed up here. Thought he was already dead, the way you look. But considering the news and your long face—he's been as good as dead anyway, right? Might as well be?"

"I can keep him alive if I can get him to New York. Doctors there. Good people. Maybe they can cure him, or at least stave off the reaper's visit. Give the man an extra ten years or so on this earth."

"Hell, that sounds like trouble. He an old man, why put him through that mud?"

"He's only fifty-two, Barney."

"Well hell! Fifty-two a hundred and two in cowboy years, you know that. Bastard's lucky enough to be living after all we done."

He tapped his chest with both hands. "Lucky enough to be alive myself! Already running on borrowed time, I feels."

"I owe him. You know that."

Barney sighed, hung his head some. "Well, you may be right. May be right some." He looked up, life suddenly sparkling in his eyes. As if he was ready to saddle up, hop back on his horse, and ride off on some adventure, toward a dying sun, in order to help out his old friend. "So, how can I help?"

"Well, first," Nellie said, tapping the table, "you helping mighty fine with the food and board."

"That all?"

"We on a hunt," she said through a sly smile.

"Mmm. Hunting, huh? Well hell, you hunting dinosaurs or outlaws? A bit of both?"

"Outlaw this time," Nellie said. "Man named Francis Burner."

Barney didn't respond right away, and the silence seemed to drag. He'd heard of Burner. Finn would have bet his last nickel on such.

"Burner, huh?" A low, hearty chuckle. "Francis fuckin' Burner."

"Heard of him?" Charlie asked, and suddenly Charlie seemed very interested in what the man had to say, more so than he had over the course of the last ten minutes. He seemed to become agitated, as if the mere mention of this legendary villain were ragged splinters under his fingernails.

"Heard of him?" Barney freed an incredulous chuckle. "Not too many people haven't. Hell, you got ears, odds are most people living that frontier life heard of Francis Burner. Nasty motherfucker, he is."

"He killed Charlie's wife and kid," Nellie said plainly.

Charlie's eyes grew a little wet at the blatant mention.

"Awwww..." Barney said, his brow softening as empathy

made its rounds across his face, as well as Martina's. "...Well hell, sorry to hear that, Charlie."

"Happened a decent time ago," Charlie said. "Still not over it, but...you know...each day is a little better. It'll be much better once the son of a bitch is gone and buried for good. Thought he was dead up until a few days ago."

"Yeah, men like Francis Burner never truly die, though. Do they?"

Charlie seemed to meditate on those words, a haunted look touching his face. "No, I guess they don't. The ghosts of bad men seem to live on forever."

"Indeed so," Barney said. "Known a lot of bad ones too. And, in ways I cannot properly describe, they do still haunt me."

"Well..." Charlie raised his beer, the amber drink still bubbling. "To the ghosts that plague us."

"To the ghosts," Barney agreed.

And they all tapped their glassware.

THEY SLEPT like babies on a windless night. Come morning, Charlie was the first to rise. He dipped into his private stash of tobacco and filled his pipe, smoked away the morning hours watching the sun rise and the sky fill with magenta splashes that fought back the night. It was full morning, a true-blue overhang, when Nellie emerged from the cabin. She looked well rested and no longer hungry. The trail life weathered the bones, the muscles, sure, but it also spoiled the soul too. This was a brand-new Nellie Watts staring at him now.

"You look like the man of your life just bent his knee and asked to be your husband," he said to her.

"Shit, Charlie. Ain't no man ever done that, and ain't no man ever gonna do that, either."

"You certain about that?"

She grinned like she couldn't help hiding it. "Bet my last coin on it. Beautiful sunrise this morning?"

"Look at you, changing the subject." He nodded at the horizon. "She was beautiful, yes. Been a long time since I just got to...watch it, you know? Like, really appreciate the beauty of it."

"Well, glad to hear it. Hey, listen."

"What is it?"

"Barney's gonna ride with us a ways. Not all the way to *Pteranodon* Canyon, but he's going to get us back on course."

"Back on course?" He knocked his pipe on a nearby tree, shaking loose the spent, ashy contents within. "What do you mean? I have a map, the route all jotted out."

"I showed the map to Barney, and he thinks he can shave a whole day off the ride if we take his way."

"A shortcut?"

She nodded.

He sighed, chewing on the idea of listening to a stranger over his own eye and hand. "Ain't gonna claim I'm an expert of these parts, but my route is good. I know it."

"I do too. Just...with my father, in the shape he is. Every day counts, you know."

"Aye. Listen, I trust you. I trust that you trust Barney Reeves. He and Martina appear like lovely folk and their hospitality goes unrivaled. But...he's a man I don't fully know more than a night, and a man you haven't known in over a thousand nights."

"What are you saying?"

Packing himself another smoke, he shrugged. There was a second of hesitation; he'd already smoked so much his chest was beginning to grow a dull pain, but the pending conversation would surely warrant another dozen hits from the pipe. "Saying three years can change a man."

She stepped through the curtain of pipe smoke that stood between them, all so he couldn't avoid her eyes. "That man saved my life more times than I can count. You think he'd mean me harm? You honestly expect me to believe that?"

Charlie shook his head. "No, don't think that. Not at all. Well, maybe. Shit—maybe he doesn't mean harm to you at all."

"Charlie, you're not making a bull-dick's worth of sense right now." Her upper lip arched. "I expect you to speak true, sir. Right now. Out with it."

"I'm just speaking, Nellie. I don't mean anything by it. But I'll tell you this—I've gotten on good and long in this world by trusting my instincts—you know, that feeling in the belly that awakes when something appears not as it should. And...well...a man who suggests he can shave a full day off a ride from a route that I feel mighty confident about...well, that just raises more than a few suspicions." Before she could contest this, he said, "Now, now. I know what you're saying and, furthermore, I know what you're thinking. Barney Reeves is a good man with not a nefarious bone in his body, and I believe that, I do. But sometimes...the gut sees us through."

"The gut sees us through?" She looked like she might spit on him. Lob a huge ball of snot right atop his head. But she didn't. Instead, she gritted her teeth behind a twitching upper lip. "What did your gut tell you when you put your wife and kid on that train seven years ago."

Charlie didn't have much of an answer for this other than,

"You're comparing rocks and sticks, sweetheart, and I don't much appreciate that kind of talk."

"I don't appreciate yours."

"Look—let's strike a bargain. You think about what I said, about this scenario—you think it over real good. And if, at the end of this reflection, you think we should go ahead and take Barney Reeves up on his offer, then I'll saddle up and let the old cowboy take the lead. But if any part of you agrees with me..."

She swallowed what was probably another contentious phrase, another arrow for Charlie Archer's already-bleeding heart. "Get your saddle ready, cowboy. We leave at noon."

Charlie nodded. Just like that.

BARNEY LED them through the mountains, a network of cavernous tunnels that wasn't easy on the horses' hooves or their riders' backs. But once they made it across the other side, it was pretty smooth sailing across some flattened meadows, the occasional wooded pathway, and through some babbling streams. They saw a pack of *Ankylosauruses* watching as two males challenged each other for the lead position of their herd. As they engaged in battle, Finn slowed down to watch the whole thing unfold. It was an informative sight, seeing the two animals take each other on, bashing themselves with the bulbous spikes attached to the ends of their tails, hammering the impenetrable shells that shielded their bodies from almost all harm. The longer he watched, the more he suspected the fight would end in a stalemate, and he wondered how the rest of the herd would assess a crowned winner. It wasn't like he could ask them, and it wasn't like he could linger and watch the end of the battle, the behavior of the herd that would follow.

He supposed he wanted to do that one day. Just sit on his horse or high up in a tree...and watch. Watch the dinosaurs and jot down notes about their behaviors and patterns, things that separated them from other packs and herds, other species that populated the Great American West. He wondered what would happen if he wrote a book about these sorts of musings. Would someone pay him for it? The pay—even small—would sure beat traveling around and working menial jobs, jobs that didn't pay worth a spit. Working to break his back, working for heinous men like Billy-Boy Tanner.

"Come on, Finn," Charlie called back to him. "Falling behind. Pay those animals no mind. That's just how they pass the time."

Finn agreed with everything but that last statement. That wasn't how the *Ankylos* passed time; it was how they learned who to follow.

A FEW CLICKS NORTH, Barney brought them to a stop. They were resting on a ridge, looking out across a wide and seemingly endless valley. *Brachiosaurs* lumbered across the green blanket of earth, shaking the entire world. Charlie could feel the tremble, and the horses felt it too. They began to dance on the rock, backing away from the source of the low-level quake.

"Easy now," Charlie called to his gelding. "Eaaaaaasy."

Not long after, the horses became used to the vibrations. Charlie wondered if those massive creatures were going to break the planet in some way with all that stomping. He supposed they might.

"Well hell," Barney said, looking at a sun that was nearing its time. An hour later and the dark would begin its slow rise. "This is where I get off. *Yellow Valley.* It's a straight shot back to that trail you done mapped out. Shaved a day off that trek, for sure."

"Well, I appreciate the information and the guidance," Charlie said, feeling badly about accusing him of anything. He didn't like to think the worst of people, but Charlie had seen his fair share of evil, and, more often than not, that was where his mind tended to travel. It was a harsh way to be, but like he'd told Nellie—there was a reason why he'd been able to do what he'd done and still be alive to continue doing it.

"No sweat," Barney told them. "Anything for the beautiful and breathtaking, Elinor 'Nellie' Watts."

Nellie laughed this off, shook her head. "You're sure a crazy old man to say such things, Barn."

"Come here and give an old cowboy one last hug."

She climbed off her horse, and he climbed off his. The two embraced, and Charlie felt a general love between them, the way a father loves his daughter, the way a daughter loves her daddy.

Charlie's throat tightened with a thick knot.

"You ride on safely, all right?" Barney told her, some tears in his eyes. "You hear me? All of you. Look after this girl...make sure nothing bad happens to her."

"You have my word," Charlie said, "though I think it's her who looks after us."

"Maybe that's true," he said, crying now. "But you look after her all the same."

"Maybe we'll see each other again, Barn," she said, patting his jacket's shoulder. "Maybe this isn't goodbye forever."

"Well, it sure feels like it, don't it? Don't know if I'll be alive in another three years, the next time you come out here and decide you need something from me." The words were harsher than his voice suggested. There was no hidden intent in them, not a speck. After, he kissed her forehead. "You save your daddy, you hear. He a good man. Best I've ever known. Saved my life, he did. Didn't owe that man a goddamn thing and he saved my life."

"I'll save him. I promise."

Barney's voice went squeaky, like a child's stuffed squeezable noisemaker. "You make sure."

After their final goodbyes, they waved Barney off as he disappeared back the way they'd come.

Charlie gave them a quick break before he took the lead again, and then guided them down the ridge, toward the valley, toward new uncertainties, whatever this bold earth would throw at them next.

MARINA WAS WAITING for him when he stepped through the cabin's front door. Seated at the table, somber in her stillness, she glared at her husband. "Why'd you do it? You could have saved them."

With tears in his eyes, Barney Reeves didn't speak a word. Instead, he bounded off to bed and cried himself to sleep, a sleep that came in waves. And when he did finally trespass into the world of slumber, he was met with dreams, terrible ones, the kind that caused him to rise up to lucidity screaming so bad his throat burned. And the architect of these dreams? The demon known as Francis Burner.

The devil with the red eyes.

His infernal master.

FRANCIS BURNER PEELS *an ace off the top of the deck and grins so wide his dry lower lip cracks, begins to bleed. He finishes out the hand, winning the uncontested pot, and then asks if everyone seated at the table wants to play again. Most of them look on with a somber reluctance, as if they have little choice in the matter and Burner's question was of the perfunctory kind. The dealer distributes the next hand, and the men draw their new cards, and again, Burner draws another ace. Two of them actually. It must be his lucky day. He's never seen so many aces fall into his favor. Again, he takes down the pot, and his*

opponents—all four of them—shift uncomfortably in their seats. Still...they don't leave.

"Couple a bad beats, huh, gents?" Burner says, laughing that smoky laugh. "Tell me something—is this some sort of arrangement?" He doesn't let them answer the question. Instead, he folds his hands on the table as if preparing for storybook time. "I can't help but figure this game here is a farce. That no matter what happens, I'm going to draw an ace—or in some cases—two or three of them. Now look, I know I'm pretty as a couple of Tyrannosaur titties, but y'all don't have to give me that much respect. I see this face in the mirror every day, and I know. I'm acutely aware of my reputation. I know some of y'all piss your johns when you see me cross the street in your direction, fearful that I'm coming for ya, fearing that your very name might leave my mouth and that would signal the end of you."

Everyone in the establishment has turned toward him now. The craps table has stopped rolling. Blackjack games have come to an abrupt stop. The patrons at the bar cease their nightly routines and now face the legendary Francis Burner as he holds court before them all.

"But I do not like being catered to, nor do I appreciate the efforts of y'all trying to suckle at my teat like piglets latching onto their momma's milk bags, each trying to squash each other to get a taste of that sweet, nourishing titty-drink. Sycophants are not welcome here. When I'm here, among you all, laughing and drinking and having my jollies, I do not want any preferential treatment. Is that understood?"

Their silence was considered an agreement.

"Well, good. Glad we got that out of the way." Burner taps the table. "Deal another."

The cards are distributed amongst the players. He sees the dealer's deck-holding hand is shaking, the nerves having some sort of spastic episode. He almost tells him not to worry, that Francis Burner can handle a losing hand. Hell, if he lost every available chip in front of him, that wouldn't be such a big deal. Would it? He doesn't think so.

He's not that angry. He's not that harsh. Francis Burner is a benevolent leader, isn't he?

Burner trades in three cards, gets three new ones.

All of them aces.

He puts down the five-card hand, faces up, showing off this incredible draw. A pain enters the center of his brain. Needle-like. Repeated stabbing. Over and over, again and again, until there is only the constant painful rip that severs his thoughts and pollutes his mind.

Before he knows what he's doing, his gun is drawn, and he's aiming it at the dealer's head.

A loud pop. Brains on the wall.

Everybody flinches but nobody moves. Nobody makes for the door. Nobody dares.

"Tanner!" Burner calls.

Billy-Boy Tanner emerges from the darkened corner, where he was sitting by his lonesome, nursing a glass of whiskey. "Yes, sir?"

"Clean up this mess. And then find me a new dealer. One that doesn't know how to deal from the bottom of the deck."

"Yes, sir," Tanner says, and then hustles off to make good on his promise.

4

GORED MAN * BEAUTIFUL CREATURES II * RAPTORS OF
THE ROCKY RIDGE * DREAM SMOKE * SUNSETS AND
DEATH

Charlie pulled strips of *T. rex* jerky out from his saddle bag and handed them out, three each. He'd bought the stuff back at the last general store they had hit, about three clicks south. The trio had filled up on several needs —blankets for the horses, snacks for the trail, a few canisters of dino repellent for those nights spent out in the open, and, of course, ammo. Regarding the latter, they had completely cleaned out the store of their inventory, and Charlie was uncertain that the shopkeeper would actually sell them that much. But they had laid out the cash on the counter, and once the owner saw they meant business and planned to pay for every bullet, well—there was no way he could say "no." He had asked if they planned on going on a shooting spree there in town, a question Charlie laughed off in the most uproarious fashion.

But the man behind the counter didn't find the notion as funny as Charlie had, which got Charlie thinking maybe there had been a shooting incident or two in the past. Either way, it made no difference in terms of the sale, and the three waltzed out of there fully loaded, enough firepower to take down a dozen *T. rexes* should they run into some nesting grounds. Charlie didn't believe that would happen, though. Barney Reeves would have made mention of any potential wildlife hazards along the road ahead.

He was sure of that.

After they stopped for a jerky break, they hit the trail again. About a mile later, they were stopped by a fellow traveler, a young boy who looked like he'd gone and caught himself in a mud storm. Brown smears painted his face and arms, and clung to his clothing. The way he stunk made Charlie wonder if he'd charged head-first into a pile of *rex* dung. The boy waved his hands over his head frantically, as if whatever situation that required their help was a matter of life and death.

"Hey there, youngster," Charlie said, bringing his horse to a stop. "What can we do you for?"

"My paw!" he shouted, jumping, terror gripping his face.

"Your daddy? What's wrong with him?"

"Wagon flipped...he..." The boy bent over, put both hands on both knees, and gasped for a hurried breath. He'd clearly been running for the better part of his journey over here. "We got caught...in a stampede."

"Your wagon flipped?" Finn asked. "Your paw okay?"

"No!" he shouted. "Come on!"

Charlie looked at the other two, wondering if each of them were thinking the same damn thing—that this was a ruse, perhaps one of the oldest in the book. Something the McClellan gang might have pulled off when one of them was young enough to portray the innocence of a small, frightened child.

"How do we know you're for real?" Finn asked first.

"Please...my paw! You have to help him! Or he may die and leave me an orphan!"

"He may die anyway," Charlie said, "and still leave you an orphan."

"You're wastin' time!"

"Now hold on, young buck." Charlie nodded to his group, asking for a private conference. Once the three were far enough so the boy could not hear them, he asked, "What do we make of this?"

Finn was the first to react. "Don't like it, for more than a few reasons. Chief among them is that it smells like fish."

Charlie faced Nellie. "And you?"

She seemed to study the boy. Charlie looked back in his direction, and he noticed the kid bouncing on his heels as if he were holding in a long pee. He kept checking the woods every three seconds or so as if the trees had teeth and they were hungry.

"Seems legit," she replied. "And if not, hats off to the boy for being a fantastic actor."

"We helping?" Finn asked.

Charlie sighed. Any chore that wasn't directly involved with their trip to *Pteranodon* Canyon could set them back days, and Smitty's offer didn't last forever. He figured they had until all the flying reptiles were poached, and who knew how long that was. Every second not spent riding toward the canyons was a wasted one, and that could cost them their purse. Plus, there was Nellie's father to consider.

"You call it, Nell," he said. "Your father being sick and all, figure any delay affects you the most."

She considered it. The boy continued to wave at them, jumping up and down, calling out for their immediate assistance.

"Suppose it's just a flipped wagon," she said. "Would take, what? A couple hours to rectify?"

"That's if it's just turning over a wagon and not something else," said Finn, the voice of pessimism. "Suppose the man's already dead. Or worse—let's say he's attracted some pack hunters. And that's if the whole thing's legit. I mean...I know you didn't ask for it, but I say this is a mess we don't want to find ourselves entangled in."

Charlie considered his words. "Like the mess with the McClellan boy? That kind of mess?"

Finn shook his head as if he had known his earlier confession would come back to bite him.

"Make the call, Nell," Charlie said again.

"All right. We ride out with him. See what the damage is and if there's anything we can do to help. We catch a whiff of something foul along the way, we bail faster than a duckbill stumbling across a *rex* nest."

"All right," Charlie said. "You heard the woman. Let's ride out."

THE BOY RODE with Nellie and she didn't mind; the kid shouted directions to the fallen wagon in her ear, and she steered the course. Through the woods, about two clicks, and they came out into an open field, the grass taller than a stagecoach driver would typically like to coast through. She didn't see a viable path that would lend itself to a wagon or stagecoach, and this automatically raised her suspicion. She brought her horse to a gradual pace, something slower than a trot. Glancing over her shoulder, she asked the kid, "Where's your pa's wagon?"

"Just up ahead," he said. "I swear it. Ain't pullin' your leg."

"Better not be, kid," she said, "or it will mean death for you and your associates." She wasn't kidding either. Though she certainly wouldn't blame the kid completely if the plot turned out to be some nefarious one—rather, she'd place the fault on the elder cohorts—she still couldn't guarantee that she wouldn't put a bullet in him out of pure anger for executing such a swift scheme. It was best to warn him now, allow him the opportunity to fess up. "Tell me now and tell me true—this a trick?"

"No trick. No, ma'am."

"Very well."

She sped up and cruised over to where the kid's tongue directed. Once closer, she saw there was indeed a wagon, and indeed it was flipped on its side. There was no visual on the driver, the kid's pa.

The kid leapt from the horse in mid-stride, which Nellie thought was a risky maneuver. She'd seen grown men snap an ankle attempting lesser stunts.

"Paw?" the kid said, running over to the wagon, his voice strained, full of wild panic. "Paw? Paw? Where are you, paw-paw? Answer me!"

"Calm down, kid!" Finn shouted. "You trying to attract the big ones? Sheesh."

But the kid didn't calm down. He only raised his voice, became more animated. "Paw-paw!" Tears filled his eyes and began to drip. "Where is he?"

"Where was he before?" Charlie asked, dismounting.

"He was trapped under the wagon. And unconscious. Couldn't pull him out."

Nellie hopped off her horse and walked around the crash site, inspecting underneath the crushed wagon and around the immediate area. No sign of any man, and the wagon, well...the way it was all smashed in on itself, looking like a wood-boarded house caught in the aftermath of a wicked tornado—no one could have lived through that kind of damage.

Finn examined the prints stamped in the earth. "*Triceratops.* Whole herd of them from the looks of it."

"They crashed into us!" the kid said. "One of them flipped us! I got out and scrambled into the woods...but paw...he was trapped inside."

Finn was the first one brave enough to scope out the validity of this claim, the first one who tried to confirm the dead body.

"Well...?" Nellie paced back and forth, waiting in anticipation, waiting for confirmation of the very thing she already knew deep down in her gut. "You see him?"

Finn rose, a misfortunate look softening his features. "No body, unless he was crushed flat and buried beneath the dirt."

"Highly unlikely," Charlie added.

"Indeed." Finn scanned the trees. "Maybe he was lucky enough to get out."

"Maybe something dragged him out," Nellie mused, reaching for her holster.

"Maybe." Finn investigated the dirt and trampled grass around the wagon for more clues, bending down and running his fingers along the indents and smushed earth.

While he was doing this, Nellie turned to Charlie. "Guess the kid wasn't lying."

"Told you I wasn't," the kid snapped.

Charlie stared the boy down a bit, as if there were possibly other lies to uncover. "What's your name, kid?"

"Davey," he said.

"Davey what?"

"Davey Hill, sir."

"And your father?" Charlie asked. "What's his name?"

"Wyatt."

"Wyatt and David Hill," Charlie said as if the names sounded familiar on his tongue, though his face gave no inclination of recognition. "Well, we'll look for your daddy. But we are pressed for time, so if we can't find him, we'll drop you off at the nearest town so the local lawmen can take over. How's that sound, Davey?"

"Please find him."

"I reckon we'll do our best."

Finn invited the rest of the group over for a small conference. Davey wasn't invited but he came anyway, and no one had the heart to tell him that the words about to be spoken were only for adult ears, that the words might contain truths he wasn't ready for. Nellie's heart broke for the now father-less kid, and it got her thinking about her own father, how she'd never spent nearly enough time with him, how she was always running off on her own, seeking freedom and the open trail. How he couldn't control her, though he had done his best and, when she thought about it, he was actually a really good parent, the best she probably could have asked for in this world. And now he was almost gone. Dead, or dying—she didn't know for sure that he hadn't passed yet. For all she knew, she could ride back into Kansas after this whole *Pteranodon* Canyon business was over and find out he had passed at the beginning of her journey. Wouldn't *that* be a horse's kick in the tit?

"It's come to my attention," Finn said, his hands on his hips, still continuing to eye the evidence the field provided, "that Mr. Wyatt Hill might still be alive."

"Really?" Davey's face lit up like the surface of a lake on a sunny noon. "Really? You mean it?"

"I do, but I'm not certain enough to call it just yet. We have to follow the trail."

"The trail?"

Finn pointed to a small patch of pressed grass and displaced dirt. *Triceratops* prints were easily identifiable enough, and even Nellie knew the beasts had stomped through here.

"Leads in that direction. Looks like your paw must have scrambled out before the herd trampled over this here wagon."

"So, he's alive? Oh, boy! Is he really?"

"Don't get your hopes up, son," Charlie said. "This could end a thousand different ways, and most of them probably end in your father's untimely passing. So don't fill yourself with false hopes."

The kid's face melted into a mask of worry.

Nellie put her arm around him. "It's okay. If he is alive, we'll find him."

And so, Finn led them along the tracks, the human tracks that took them to the edge of the forest, between two trees.

One of the trees was marked by blood.

Fresh blood.

Human.

THEY FOLLOWED the blood trail down to the river where a man lay on the banks, holding his gut as if he was trying to prevent everything inside from spilling out. When they got closer, Charlie could see that was exactly the case. Red painted the front of him, covering everything from his shirtless stomach to his torn britches. The bloodshed was enormous for just one body.

"Paw!" Davey shouted, breaking free from the group and sliding down the bank.

Charlie called after him, wanting the kid to stop, but the kid kept on running, and Charlie supposed he couldn't blame him. Had it been his own father down there on the sandy decline with his guts hanging out, he might have rushed over there too.

Davey reached his old man and wrapped his arms around his neck, bawling into his shoulder. The kid's old man hugged him back lazily, his arms shaking with the knowledge that he was nearing the end of his time on this earth, that before long a gray shrouded figure would emerge from the murky depths of the underworld and lay claim to his soul. The way the man stared on, past the river, past the trees, Charlie thought he might already be seeing that figure.

Slowly, the three gunslingers made their way down the embankment, to the muddy shores of the calm, trickling brook. Once their boots were firmly planted, they approached the man with a certain amount of caution, as if he were carrying some sort of rabid disease. Charlie was the first to kneel down beside him and observe the damage done to his midsection. He didn't really need the man to remove his hands from the wound to get an idea of what was behind them, but he motioned for Wyatt Hill to do so anyway.

"Let me take a look, Mr. Hill," he said.

The man glared at him as if Charlie were here to loot his innards.

"You can trust him, Paw," Davey said. "They rode out a good ways to help. Good people, they are."

The boy's word seemed good enough for his father, and Wyatt removed his hands from the injury. What Charlie set his eyes on turned his stomach, and Charlie considered himself a tough man, a man who'd seen many gruesome injuries and stomached them all. But this one seemed worse somehow. There was a ragged hole that burrowed deep into his gut, about the circumference of a can of peas. When Wyatt's hands were no longer plugging it, pinkish parts threatened to poke out, as if they were peeking into the world outside before fully committing to the fall.

"All right," Charlie said, taking the man's bloody hands and folding them back over the wound. "Got yourself a good one there." Charlie checked the man's back, saw an additional hole, saw it was actively bleeding, but at least vital organs weren't attempting to escape through that one. The amount of blood leaking was concerning, however. "Guessing a *Triceratops* horn got to you?"

The shivering man nodded the best he could.

"Very well." Charlie turned to the others. "Half-minded to move him. The other half is saying, why waste the energy? He's as good as dead if we don't get him to a doctor in the next hour, I'd say."

Nellie reached behind her to grab Charlie's map, which she'd borrowed and never returned. "Next town, according to this, isn't within that range."

"Well, shoot."

"No!" Davey cried, and he swiped at the tears running from his eyes in bunches. "No! You have to try!"

Charlie kneeled next to him. "Son, you have to be reasonable here. No sense in wasting time and energy getting your pa up that mudbank, putting him through more agony if he's just going to expire anyways."

"NO!"

"I know it's rotten business this thing called death, and I wish it wasn't so. But let this be a lesson to you. The teaching is this: this world is cold and sometimes there just ain't no warmth, no matter how many layers you pile on or how many fires you start—the world is just damn cold."

The lesson he bestowed upon the kid seemed to sink in rather quickly, and Davey turned his body to look down on his father one last time. The old man's eyes rolled and rolled, and, at that moment, Charlie could see the kid understood what he'd said—there was no way they could get the man to a doctor in time to save his life.

"Wish we could save him, kid," Finn added out of some self-obligation to comment on the current state of things.

They stood with the man and boy for a few minutes. The boy whispered prayers and hugged his pa while the three watched on, reflecting on their own lives, their own loved ones, and their current lives without those important people in them. At least that's what Charlie did. He couldn't speak for the others, but the looks on their faces clued him in on one thing—they were all entrenched in deep thought, of times past.

In a few minutes, the light in the man's eyes began to burn out. Fading. Drifting toward the certain darkness that would one day claim them all.

And then a light spell of thunder shook the world beneath them.

NELLIE GLANCED up from the dying (or now dead) man. Near the end of the brook, where it took a wide turn up north, stood a massive *Triceratops*. The beast watched the group for a minute before it took to pacing and stamping its left foot in the mud, as if planning to launch itself at an enemy invader.

And that's exactly what they were to it—enemies. Invaders. Must have been what the Hills' wagon appeared to be, the reason why they were attacked. Nellie didn't know a whole lot about the species but knew enough to know that this one felt threatened. And when a *Triceratops* felt threatened, it attacked with a ferociousness reserved for instinctive killers.

This one seemed to be foaming from the mouth and extraordinarily aggressive.

"Don't move," Finn said from the corner of his mouth. "Don't move a damn muscle."

"You kidding?" Nellie asked. "Best shot we have is to scramble for those trees."

"You make a move, and that thing will gore you before your fingers can reach the bark." Finn stood firm. "Don't. Move."

"I can make it."

"Nellie," Charlie said, the way a parent might scold a child threatening to do something dangerous.

The *Triceratops* continued to pace, rubbing the stubby point of its nose on the ground, muddying itself up. Foam like ale head continued to leak from its mouth.

"This one is sick, extra angry," Finn stated, but Nellie had already drawn that conclusion from the aggressive nature it displayed, coupled with the peculiar actions it took with the front horn. It was as if it knew it was ill and it was trying to rub off the illness on the ground. "It will get you."

"I can make it," Nellie insisted. "Provide a distraction."

"You'll get yourself killed, woman," Finn said. "Don't be stubborn headed, not now. We already got one body to bury, don't make it two."

But she was hardly listening to him anymore. Instead, she was scanning the trees along the embankment, picking out the most climbable trunk. She found one with branches that hung every six feet or so, and the closer to the top, the more options there were to pull herself up. She had climbed trees a lot when she was a kid, and the one that was luring her looked just like the ones from her youth, the exact kind she used to mount the top of and look out across the vast green forests, pretending she was as tall as some hungry sauropod.

That tree was it. That was the one.

Before Finn could continue to list out all the reasons she shouldn't, Nellie took off for the muddy incline. She dug her hands into the soft earth, gripping the exposed roots, and pulled herself up. Her left foot found purchase in the slippery slope, but the right foot couldn't follow suit and slid, kicking back her whole body. "Shit!" she cried out and then looked over her shoulder to check the status of the charging beast.

It was already on the move, snorting and making some noise that sounded like an enraged demon horse from Hell.

On her second attempt, she was able to jump and grab the exposed roots higher up where the earth had eroded less over the last century or so, but enough to where she could still hold on and support her weight. Using her considerable strength, she kicked at the mud, half-slipping but finding enough grip to hoist herself up. In less than the amount of time it took for a horse to gallop ten paces, she was up the bank and sprinting for the tree. Over her shoulder, she saw the *Triceratops* taking to the climb. It was slowed by the wet earth, but not enough to make Nellie feel anywhere near safe. As she reached the base of the tree and put one hand on the first branch, the *Triceratops* had completed the climb and was already lowering its head for battle. She moved up the tree quite easily, much more gracefully than she had imagined.

The *Triceratops* charged the tree, and Nellie braced herself for impact. The first collision sounded off with a loud crack, a sound she didn't want to hear, a sound that told her this tree was coming down. She hadn't prepared for that. She thought once she was up high, the animal would leave her alone to go wander the forest in search of other creatures to terrify. But no—this thing was determined. It backed up several paces, then charged again, leaping this time to put some extra velocity into the punch.

The tree swayed, the sounds of the lumber coming apart as loud as a bullwhip hitting the tough flesh of its target.

She quickly analyzed the rest of the trees, trying to predict which way her support would fall. She hoped it would fall in the direction of another one and not toward an empty section, like toward the bank. A fall to the bottom of the bank would be too great, and although she might have a chance at hitting the earth without breaking a bone, it wasn't likely. The water that ran through the gully was only ankle-high, maybe hip-high in parts, but certainly not deep enough to soften a tumble from this height.

The dinosaur charged again, and, this time, she felt the tree shift, and her equilibrium tilt as the entire world warped and spun away from her.

CHARLIE AND FINN reacted as soon as the tree trunk cracked off. They both knew what had happened upon hearing the noise, and neither bothered to turn to the kid and inform him of their intentions—they just moved as quickly as possible up the bank in a similar manner to what Nellie had done, grabbing the exposed tree roots and pulling themselves up.

Charlie knew Nellie had been impetuous, and even though her intentions were born from a good place, he couldn't be more pissed off that she'd gone and done a thing like that. He unholstered his weapons as soon as he reached the top of the bank and aimed at the thick-bodied beast, fully intending to put the sick creature out of its misery. Killing herbivores brought him zero pleasure—killing most animals brought him no pleasure, if he was being honest—but he kept telling himself that the poor creature needed a quick death in order to be released of the demonic illness that had claimed its soul.

Before he could fire, the tree trunk snapped in half, and he watched Nellie fly through the air, her back toward the ground. The movement must have caught her off guard because she flailed her arms and legs, desperately reaching out for something to hold on to, or something that would make her fall to the earth a little less violent. But there didn't seem to be anything except open air, and he knew the impact was going to ruin her.

Charlie concentrated on the *Triceratops* because the fall was going to be bad enough without having a charging three-horned animal there to meet her. He shot at it, aiming for the plated crest that protected the vulnerable area behind its head. Finn joined in, firing shot after shot, hitting the shield of the head that contained the tri-horns slicked with mud and—now that they were close enough to see—splashes of drying blood. Wyatt's blood most likely. And suddenly Charlie could envision what had caused the stampede that had eventually ended Wyatt Hill's life. Maybe one, or more, in the herd was sick and had started attacking its friends, and the next thing you knew there was a herd of Triceratops running for their lives, the well trying to separate themselves from the ill.

It seemed true enough.

The bullets didn't seem to do much. While the gunslingers reloaded, the Triceratops swung its ugly head in their direction, leaving Nellie be for the moment. Charlie stole a glance at the fallen tree and wondered if it had come down on top of her, crushing her like a mosquito underneath the hand of its human victim. Charlie was reloaded in almost no time, and he aimed at the head. Two shots sunk into the leathery-gray flesh, but that did nothing as the creature dragged its foot along the earth, preparing to charge. It let out another feral cry and launched itself like a bull rider from the gate after the horn sounds. Charlie expected the beast to come after him and was surprised when it chose Finn as its target. Finn seemed surprised too because he fumbled his reload, dropped shells to the earth and stumbled to pick them up. The *Triceratops* reached him with surprising quickness, and Finn had no choice but to jump in the air and hope to avoid getting gored by one of the two long horns. The *Triceratops* flicked his massive head, connecting with Finn's body, and launched Finn into the air. Finn cried out with utter shock and a bit of pain. Charlie couldn't see if one of the horns had gotten him, but the aerial ascension seemed scary enough to warrant such a cry.

Charlie saw Finn disappear down the bank, toward the running water below. Momentum took the beast over the side, and the animal slid down the decline after him.

Charlie wasn't sure which situation was more important to solve first—Nellie's or Finn's. He opted for Finn's since he was probably injured and was in close proximity to the rabid beast. Even though the uncertainty of Nellie's condition worried him, if she *was* hurt, there was nothing he could do immediately to mend her. But Finn, on the other hand, was still in the middle of death's dance and Charlie had a chance to rescue him from that eternal tango.

He neared the edge of the bank and looked down. Finn had landed in the center of the river, and, although he looked a little rough, there were no visible wounds on his body. It seemed he'd dodged the horns. He was climbing back to his feet when the *Triceratops* bull found his. Only, it had abandoned its pursuit of Finn and concentrated on its next target—it looked like it wanted to finish what it'd started.

It stomped its feet, and then barreled toward Wyatt Hill's corpse and the youngster clinging to his dead father for dear life.

Nellie opened her eyes, surprised she was still in the woods. She had expected to open them to an eternal black, or—not that she believed in such afterlives—some fiery inferno where she was damned to exist in perpetuity. But nope. The forest surrounded her, towering oaks and redwoods alive and still green from an extended summer, and even though the nights were cooler heading into autumn, they still clung to that sage hallmark.

She pushed herself up, feeling surprisingly well, as if she'd fallen into a bed of fluffy pillows rather than the mass grave of pine needles that littered the hard, packed earth. She had avoided being crushed by the downed trunk by mere feet. The tree's carcass lay to her right, splintered near the base.

There was some doubt about her condition, but once she got to her feet and tested her muscles, and the bones they were attached to, she realized how lucky she had actually been. Nary a bruise on her body. It was like she had been placed softly on the ground by some caring angelic force.

Once she was certain there wasn't a single thing wrong with her, she looked for her guns, both of which had slipped from their holsters and were now scattered somewhere in the forest. It only took a quick glance to locate them, as they had not strayed too far from where she'd made impact.

She grabbed them and headed for the embankment.

Upon looking down, she noticed two things: Finn was hurt and the boy they had helped locate the father of was in the wrong spot at the wrong time.

The *Triceratops* sped off after the boy and his fallen father. If the kid's old man wasn't dead, he was surely past the point of no return. As the animal hurled itself toward them, he didn't move a muscle, despite his son's plea to get moving.

In her periphery, she saw Charlie sliding down the mud-slicked bank, toward Finn. Instead of wasting seconds getting to the bottom, she opted to remain on the high ground. Aiming her dual revolvers, she fired down on the thumping *Triceratops*, the bullets hitting its thick body, stripping away flecks of tough flesh as the bullets disappeared inside the muscle. The shots didn't slow down the animal, and the boy did his best to move out of the way before the bull had the opportunity to run its horns through him. Davey leapt out of the way about three seconds before the horns were on him. Instead, the fallen father took the brunt of the violence, and Nellie watched with shock and disgust as the man's body was trampled over, those massive feet stamping his body into the soft, wet earth. As the enraged bull began to turn his body, she realized there wasn't much time and that, sooner or later, the kid would end up like his father, a flattened slab of broken bones and crushed muscle, organs reduced to ooze. Surprisingly, the sick animal didn't go for Davey—instead, it chose to lower its set of horns at the dead man again. It barreled forth, jumping in the air seconds before making impact, as if it wanted the collision to be as bloody and violent as possible. As the dinosaur smashed its face against the battered and bleeding body, Nellie looked on, seeing the man's head cave in like an old mango. Blood squirted from his eyes, ears, nose, and mouth, pouring like rivers of their own. The *Triceratops* ground its snout into the man's chest, opening up a brand-new hole in his body. The animal's feral, diseased grunts were heard over the snapping of bones. Like a child's rag doll at the mercy of a temper tantrum, there was nothing anyone could do but sit back and watch the savagery unfold. Foamy spittle flew from its mouth as it went back for a third and fourth round, backing up a few paces before charging forth and pulverizing the dead, brutalized body of Wyatt Hill.

"*Psst. Kid,*" Nellie said, trying to gain his attention without calling the *Triceratops's*. Horror holding his eyes hostage, he craned his head in her direction. "Get up here. Now. Double time."

The kid seemed paralyzed by what he'd just witnessed, his

face unable to respond to the cruelty the world had displayed before him. It took her several more attempts to coax him into joining her. When she finally got him moving, his strides were feeble and certainly not quick enough considering how surprisingly nimble the horned beast moved when it was motivated.

When he reached the bank, she bent down and offered her hands, pulling him up to a relatively safe place. She noticed that Charlie and Finn had managed to make the climb on the other side, and were gathering their supplies, ready to make their final stand against this poor creature. No one wanted to kill the dinosaur, but it was badly diseased and there was no bringing it back from that darkness. Now that it was officially a man-killer, there was that charge to lay upon it as well. If nothing more, it was revenge for Wyatt Hill by way of execution.

"Stand back," Nellie said, making sure the kid was shielded from the *Triceratops*, as if she wanted to make sure he was hidden in case the beast had some personal vendetta against the Hill family. She didn't think that was the case, but it was odd it'd chosen to ensure Wyatt's death rather than bull an injured Finn Hampton. Vendettas were typically of no importance in the animal kingdom, so she understood, but today might have changed her mind on the subject.

She steadied her aim, and the two men across the river followed her lead.

Six guns sung their violent songs, and when the last chorus rang out, the torment was over, and the sick dinosaur met its untimely and unfortunate end.

THEY PICKED UP THEIR EFFECTS, got back to the horses, and rode north just like Charlie's amended map told him, and although he trusted Barney's pen, he still felt uneasy about giving up control over their route in favor of a man he'd only known for a single night. He looked back over his shoulder at Nellie, the kid clinging to her. The boy rested his head on her back, staring off into some distant past, one where his father remained alive, one where his father hadn't been buried by two men and one woman he'd never even met, in the middle of the forest he'd never even been to before. The kid hadn't spoken a word since their departure and that was just fine. Charlie thought, *Let the boy deal with his old man's passing anyway he likes.*

"Think he's okay?" Finn asked.

Charlie shrugged. "Don't know how you could be after a thing like that."

"What we gonna do with him?"

Charlie looked down his nose at him. "Tell you what we ain't gonna do with him—drop him off in some town with the prayer that someone takes him in."

"I done told you—"

"I know what you told me, and I'm still bitter about it, and I might always be bitter about it, and you're gonna have to live with that. Or would you rather I draw you a second map that will take you back to Oat Creek? Huh? Just remember, Mr. Hampton, we agreed that you could come along on this trip. We don't need your guns or your experience with this Billy-Boy Tanner feller as much as you think we do."

Nellie seemed to overhear them, nodding in agreement with Charlie's statements.

"Fine," Finn said. "I'll keep my mouth shut. But I do add value to this team. I do. You hear?"

After a minute of silence, Charlie asked him, "How's the arm?"

"Not broke," Finn said tersely. Then he elaborated, as if he felt the need to. "Hurts, I guess. But definitely not broke. Broken many a bone and this one just feels tweaked."

"Beast flung you pretty high."

"I've had worse done to me. Used to ride bulls for cash back in Omaha."

"Shit, there a job you haven't held?" There was humor in this question, and it brought a smile to them all, save for the kid who continued to stare on into his own personal darkness.

"Sure seems like I've done a bit of everything. I am a wanderer of sorts. I like going to different places, doing different things." He shrugged. "Guess I like that about myself."

That last statement hinted at the possibility that that was one of only a few things Finn Hampton liked about himself.

"Tell us more about your book, Finn?" Nellie asked, a meaningless question, but one Charlie thought had the distinct purpose to stir up a conversation to pass the time. They still had a ways before they hit the next town, where they would need to secure supplies for the last leg of their trip.

"What, the dinosaur encyclopedia?" Finn shrugged. "Not much to tell on it. Haven't written it yet. I have things I'd like to tell. But I want to concentrate on the beauty of them, you know? Most people treat them as pests, dangers. But they're not. They're big and beautiful and they deserve our worship. Been here longer than us, I gather."

"Gather so," Charlie added. "Least that's what the scientists say, huh?"

"I think dinosaurs are the most beautiful thing about this world. I truly do. Killed me to shoot that *Triceratops*, but it was sick and had done terrible things, and it would have only gotten sicker and done more terrible things—I realize we were just ending its misery, and that brings comfort. I don't like killing animals less I have to."

"Only a cruel man would," Charlie said.

"Which is why I can't wait to get my hands around Tanner's throat. Because he's a cruel man, and he kills when he doesn't have to. Men and beasts alike."

"So does Francis Burner. Seems like the pair is the perfect match."

"Let's kill both men. For the beautiful creatures in this world, the ones that never had a chance to live their proper lives."

"If I had a swig of whiskey, I'd drink to that," Charlie said.

Nellie didn't speak a word, but her eyes seemed to agree, nonetheless.

BEFORE THEY REACHED the next town, they caught up to a train of wagons that were heading westward, twelve in total. The folks in charge of this party said they were heading to California. Charlie explained Davey Hill's story, recounting almost every detail, leaving out the gory bits of course, and playing up the fact they were heading into dangerous territories, no place for a youngster. A childless couple was touched by the boy's situation and offered to take him in. Davey had no other family that he knew of, declaring himself an orphan now, and agreed to go with the travelers in search of a better life, one where he wasn't alone and abandoned. Charlie felt good about the transaction and wished the boy peace moving forward.

After they watched the party move toward the dusty horizon, Charlie rallied his troupe and edged closer to *Pteranodon* Canyon. According to the map, they were approaching some mountainous terrain that would probably put some strain on the horses, and Charlie knew he had to calculate extra time to give them a rest. Pushing them out here in the open with no shade from the sun was apt to drive them to an early grave, and they couldn't risk losing one of the horses like that, not when such an outcome could be so easily prevented.

They came to a ridge and looked down at the sandy-red earth below, skeletons of long-dead dinosaurs half-protruding from the pit. Vultures circled the sky, waiting for the three riders to meet whatever terrible fate those other beasts had. Charlie didn't think those vultures would be anything but disappointed as there didn't seem to be any real dangers out here, no threats with razor-sharp teeth or claws, horns that could drill through a man, much of what they'd witnessed all along this strange and brutal journey.

He thought back to sitting in that tavern at Oat Creek across from Smitty, and the generous offer that was currently on the table. He'd been on jobs like this in the past, the long ride, the one that took a week or more to finish—it was what he was going to do after that always got him through those tough assignments. But this time he didn't have a set plan. Nothing stood on the forefront of his thoughts, no specific town called his attention. He supposed he'd return to Oat Creek—it was as good a town as any. Peaceful. Not much happened there, and that fact was sweet music to his ears. He hated to sound like such an *"old man"* about it, but it was true—he was getting too old for fisticuffs and bar-room brawls, too old to be chasing women, too old to be getting out of bed the next morning still-drunk from the night before and feeling like someone had clocked him over the head with a nail-studded timber. And he wasn't even that old, not by any average standard. He could still find a job as a town sheriff or even a mayor. Hell, with his resume, he could probably land one of those jobs quite easily.

But this job...this business in *Pteranodon* Canyon—it felt like the last one. He liked the taste of that little slice of finality.

"You see 'em?" Finn said, breaking Charlie from his thoughts.

"I see them," Nellie said.

They were walking their horses now, and Charlie couldn't recall the moment they had slowed down. He'd been *that* taken by his thoughts. "What is it?"

They turned to him, each shooting their alleged leader a sideways glance, one that seemed to question his sanity. Maybe not question it so much as require some sense of validation that it was still as sharp as it ever was.

"Where'd you go, Charlie Archer?" Nellie said in a voice meant to tease, not scold.

"Here and there," he said. "A little bit of everywhere."

"Raptors," Finn said, sticking strictly to business. "Across the ridge."

Finn nodded, and Charlie followed the invisible path his movement carved across the two ridges, the canyon below separating them from the potential danger. And there was danger, he could see that now. A pack of *Utahraptors* were feasting on a fallen *Brachiosaur*. The sauropod was a youth, no more than a year old. It must have wandered out here alone, because if it had been with the herd, it was likely the raptors wouldn't have attacked. But—here they were, four of them, feasting on the opened stomach of the downed sauropod. It was long past dead, and the raptors hardly looked up from their bountiful kill to notice the three passing bounty hunters.

"Think they see us?" Charlie asked, watching them strip the raw meat from the belly, knock their heads back, and swallow the contents between their bloodied jaws. They chirped with delight after each mouthful.

"Oh, they see us," Finn said, but not in any way to cause alarm. He was as calm as a butterfly fluttering across an open meadow. "But they're busy."

"Think it's the same pack from before?"

"Doubt it. *Utahraptors* are pretty common in this area. Let's hope they all eat as well as these four."

Charlie agreed.

The last thing he wanted was to be on their menu.

Charlie Archer was the hunter, never the bounty.

SUNDOWN HIT HARD AND FAST, and night swept over the sky, bringing with it the map of the stars, bright and ever-present. The trio decided it was best to make camp near the ridge, giving them one less direction to be snuck up on. Charlie went to sleep first; he wished them goodnight and disappeared into his makeshift tent. Within a few minutes, they could hear him snoring away as his consciousness slipped off into the world of dreams.

Finn unpacked something from his saddlebag, and, at first, Nellie thought it was some kind of late-night snack, something he'd picked up during one of their trips into town. But as he unfolded the cloth, she realized it was a pipe. She hadn't known him to be a smoker and had only seen Charlie light up once in a while, not the habitual user like her father had been. It hadn't dawned on her that the smoke might have attributed to whatever sickness was currently attacking his body, but now that the idea gripped her, she couldn't let it go.

"What you got there?" she asked between sips from her flask filled with spring water.

"Dream smoke," he said with amusement.

"Dream smoke?"

He nodded as he packed what looked like crystals into the pipe. "Bought some off elderly Indians in Nevada. You ever partake?"

"Is it like peyote?"

"Something like it, I suppose. Not a plant, though." When the pipe was packed, he allowed his eyes to linger over the product that looked, to Nellie, like bits of crushed glass. "They get it from the mountains, or at least that's what they told me."

"Is it safe?"

"Safe as peyote, I reckon."

"I don't need you wandering off when I'm on watch. Can't watch the camp *and* babysit you."

"No, this stuff puts you to sleep. The properties only cause hallucinatory projections when inside the sleep, so you see, that's why they call it dream smoke."

"Dream smoke," she repeated, as if she was getting used to the word, how it sounded on her tongue.

"Dream smoke," he said, and then took his first hit.

It didn't take long for Finn to find sleep. Aided by the natural substance mined by the western world's natives, Finn lay inside his tent, closed his eyes, and floated off into some great beyond. When he got there, he was met by a rush of colors, rainbows that moved in different directions, north and south, east and west, traveling like locomotives, passing and crashing into each other, and then the rainbows began to run like wet paint, the thin, cheap kind mixed by some amateur outfit. Finn walked through the rainbows, allowing the primary colors to bleed onto him, dab his flesh in bright yellows and reds, greens and blues. The color filled the world. He walked down the rainbow streets and directly into a rainbow saloon where he was served a rainbow beer by rainbow barmaids. Everyone inside the saloon laughed, and when their jaws relaxed, rainbows arced out from the dark pits of their mouths. Everything was rainbows but soon the rainbows bled away and became fuzzy. Finn thought he'd miss the rainbows and he begged for the dream smoke to bring them back—he was enjoying their aura. But the dream smoke didn't listen to its guest, never had, so why would it start now? The color of the world transitioned from this multi-colored universe into a foggy atmosphere that contained subdued shades of green and orange, quite the difference from those bright, exploding vibrancies. It took a moment for his dream eyes to adjust, and once they did, he realized where he was—back east, on the docks of some Rhode Island shore. At the end of the dock was a figure, and his back was facing Finn. Finn looked behind him and only saw a shadow world, a misty haze that stood like a towering wall he couldn't see over. No throughway whatsoever. Just the dock before him and the mysterious figure at the end of it. *Are you coming to see me, Finn? Oh, aren't you just?* He recognized the voice and, suddenly, he wasn't enjoying this trip the dream smoke granted him access to. It wasn't anything like his previous experiences—other trips had been more along the lines of the rainbow world, varying illusions that had brought him joy, that had opened his senses to positive alternative realities. Whatever this dark, morose environment was, he couldn't get onboard. A part of him wanted to fight the dream smoke, try to escape, but he knew what would happen to his mind if he attempted such a thing. There was a belief among dream smoke users that if you tried to resist what the smoke revealed to you, then your mind would splinter and be scattered among a thousand different places, realms that were unreachable to the sober eye. Separated into compartments that would never be accessed by any typical dreamer. In other words, the mind would be lost among the internal cosmos that lived inside all human minds. He imagined that meant he would be rendered an invalid, and would experience life as a mush-brain, vacant of all coherent thought. He didn't want that for himself, so he took what the dream smoke gave him, and even though that current fantasy was not welcomed, he had no choice. He faced the mysterious figure as it spoke, its voice buzzing like a horde of incensed wasps. *Don't you remember me, Finn? Don't you remember this face?* As soon as the figure turned, he knew who had come to ruin his trip. It was

Billy-Boy Tanner in all his one-eyed glory, the empty cavity where his ocular accessory ought to have been actively bleeding, running like the colors that had preceded this level of the dream. The blood turned black, evil. If Tanner had a soul—and all living things had one, didn't they?—Finn imagined that Tanner's bled black too, the ichor of such malignant devils. *Do you remember what you stole from me? Do you remember what you took?* Finn fought the memory, fought it good and hard, but the gray-white smoke of the dream unfurled before him, sweeping him away from that dark dock that extended out over the black Rhode Island waters. Next, he was in a dead and colorless desert, the dunes arching high above him like the skyscrapers of some lost, forbidden city occupied by an ancient civilization that had been wiped from the earth by the hands of some terminal doom. On one of the dunes, Tanner lay on his back, facing the black sun that spat noxious trails of some cosmic vapor, looking through one good eye and one eye that was not-so-good because it had been ruined, shot out, and the smoking gun was in Finn's hand. Black smoke that would burn in the angriest of fires rose out of the devastating injury, and Tanner screamed up at the colorless sea that made up the sky, cursing Finn's name repeatedly. Then a *Tyrannosaur* leaned over one of the dunes, those hungry jaws snapping, those whip-crack sounds filling the ears of the dream. The dinosaur clamped its teeth down on Tanner's body and the blood ran from the new holes those teeth created, and the blood was rainbow blood, a smorgasbord of bright primaries that the sand dune absorbed as if it was thirsty and the rainbow blood was the only thing it had sipped in ages, eons, an incalculable collection of seconds. The carnivore turned on Finn next, and as the severed limbs of Tanner's body twitched in its mouth, Finn could see the dinosaur also had one eye, and then realized it was the bull from Oat Creek, the one he'd shot up pretty good back when this whole thing had started. Before the dinosaur could get him, Finn blinked and he was back on the dock again, that silver-white and shadowed existence revealing itself twofold. Instead of Tanner at the end of the dock, it was Willy McClellan, the short-brained boy with which he'd been tasked to find a new home. Only...the boy had a hole in the center of his head and the hole was leaking rainbows, the rich liquid running down his face in a great multi-colored rivulet. He was speaking another language, perhaps one of his own creation, and his eyes had rolled completely back, hiding under his lids, revealing an all-white that made him look somewhat devilish in the backdrop of the blackwater, the colorless glow of this awful place. Finn tried to hang on, but the urge to break from the dream smoke was powerful. Still, he couldn't risk it. He wondered what he was doing on the other side of it, if he was doing anything at all. If Nellie could see him, how would he appear? Stressed? Anxious? Full-on psychotic episode, a breakdown of monumental propor-tions? Would she wake him up? Would that count the same as if he dislodged himself? Would that punish him in the same manner? So many questions he had for this dream smoke, yet they would go unanswered because the dream smoke didn't answer questions, only issued them. The boy opened his mouth and let out a strangled, gargling scream. Then something black emerged from the open cavity, something that looked like a slug or a river leech. One of those bayou suckers, thick and black and hard to remove. The kind that tore out a ring of flesh when it left the body. Then he saw it wasn't a leech at all, but, instead, a hooking claw—a raptor's dewclaw to be specific. It was as sharp as one because it cut down the boy's mouth, splitting his bottom lip and chin as easily as over-worn fabrics that had lasted decades but could no longer hold its stitching together. The boy began to split in half like a zippered costume. Rainbow streams flooded from his vertically halved body, and the docks bathed in the multi-colored flow. There was so much of it, that array of colors fanning out of the boy. It pooled onto the dock and crept toward him. The arterial spray slowed to a trickle, and then something emerged from the black waters behind the boy, something huge, hungry, with teeth, something that looked like a crocodile but bigger. Oh boy, was it bigger. The monstrous mouth opened and closed around Willy, snapping him up and dragging him back into the surrounding dark. Finn dropped to his knees in the colorful puddle that showed him no reflection. Just colors, all of them present, swirls of red, green, blue, and yellow, the colors dancing around each other in spirals. Then he began scooping up handfuls of the pigment, drinking from the offering. It was there to drink, wasn't it? Why else would it exist? It made so much sense to drink it, every last available drop. That was what the dream smoke wanted. To fill him with this power, this colorful substance that would give him abilities far beyond his own comprehension, give him everything he'd ever wanted, give him the platform so he could rise above his own mediocrity and finally trespass that special plane into—

"FINN!"

The forceful voice, that gusted like a hurricane gale, came from Nellie, and he opened his eyes to see she had her gun on him.

He blinked and found himself several hours after his experiment with the dream smoke. It wasn't dark anymore—quite the opposite. The early-morning sun had climbed over the horizon and bathed the rocks and ridge in a rich shine, tainted with strokes of tangerine and light lavender. The world was fuzzy, like one of those sepia-toned photographs, the early kind. He couldn't focus on any one thing, his vision sliding away from Nellie and over to the edge of the ridge, which wasn't far from him. Then he saw Charlie emerge from his tent, gun in hand. Then Finn's vision darted to his own body, and he realized he was naked, not a stitch on him. Sweat slicked his flesh, *hot* flesh, and he felt like he was on fire.

"What is happening?" Charlie asked, but his voice sounded different, off, much too deep to be Charlie's. It echoed as if they were in some endless cavern. "What's going on?"

"Finn," Nellie said. "He took something, and he's gone crazy."

"What?" Finn said, shaking away the after-sleep fog, trying to come down from the dream smoke, but he was stuck somewhere between here and there. "What is it? What'd I do?"

"You were doing...stuff," she said, shaking her gun at him, as if by doing so explained this said "stuff."

"I was...I was dreaming."

"You were doing more than dreaming," she told him.

Charlie approached the scene with his hands in the air, his face scrunched in confusion, clearly trying to make sense of this. "What are you saying, Nell?"

"I'm saying...he was doing...stuff...with himself."

Charlie stopped. "Come again?"

"I was dreaming," Finn said again, as if this was his only defense, as if he was not responsible for any actions that might have occurred while on the smoke. And now that he had a little more context to Nellie's accusation, he knew what she meant.

Meant that he was diddling himself.

"I don't know what happened," Finn admitted. "I've taken dream smoke loads before and nothing like that has ever happened."

"Jesus H. Christ," Charlie said, throwing up his hands in disgust. "Can you act like a professional for half a minute?"

"I've been very professional." He looked down on himself, his own shrinking member. "I mean, until this moment, I've been extremely professional...I'm professional."

"Put on your clothes and sober up," Charlie said. "I'll make breakfast."

Nellie holstered her weapon. He didn't think jerking the weasel was an excuse for shooting someone, but the way he was sweating, he figured he might have been going at it a little too vigorously for her liking, might have scared her some.

"I'm sorry, it must have been..."

(rainbows, bleeding rainbows)

"...must have been a bad trip, that's all."

She shook her head at him and walked away.

"Damn Indians," he said. "Blame them."

But no one did. No one spoke of the bad trip or the dream smoke again, and Finn decided, as long as he was in the presence of Nellie Watts and Charlie Archer, he wouldn't touch the stuff.

He would be professional.

As much as his own pitiful existence could allow.

TANNER and four men pull up to the cabin on the lake and pause to take in the beautiful scenery. It has everything you'd want in a painting that hangs over the stove—sun melting behind craggy cliffs, smearing oranges and purples across a motionless bed of water, the kept cabin nestled front and center of it all, resting beneath the birth of twilight.

At first the riders do not dismount. They linger about fifty paces from the cabin's door, watching the windows but in a calm manner, not expecting gunfire from within. If one didn't know any better, one might think this was a visit of cordial intent. But knowing Billy-Boy Tanner and the manner of his business, one could probably predict cordial was not something the man associates much with these days.

Tanner scans the windows, seeking movement inside. There is none, but, like any good hunter, he can almost smell the bodies inside, the human stink that taints the air.

"Come on out of there, man," he shouts, digging into his saddle pouch for a pinch of chew. "We got talkin' to do and ain't a lot of time to do it."

The cabin door opens a crack, and an eye appears.

Tanner smiles. "Well, hello there, lady. Your man around? Got words with him, we do."

"Go away," Marina says.

"Look, lady. You can either send him out or we can drag him out. Either way suits me fine."

The eye continues to stare at him, hard, but he returns a stare of his own a thousand times harder, and in that stare is a message: we don't want violence here today, *those eyes translate,* we don't want it, but, if it comes to it, there will be bloodshed. And lots of it. Yours, in fact.

The door swings wide and the old cowboy, the free Black man who's lived in this cabin for the past three years, sets aside his wife, pecks her on the cheek, and then steps out onto the porch, his boots clacking on the floorboards. He looks almost breathless, like he's just been jogging after some stable horses.

"I'm here, Tanner," *says Barney Reeves.* "I'm here, you cold, heartless bastard."

Spitting a long brown stream at the dirt below, Tanner grins. "Aye. So you are."

"What you doing here? I've paid my tax to the Burner man. He's got his hands in my pockets. Don't owe him a donkey's dick, I don't."

"You know why I'm here," *Tanner says.* "Telegraph you done sent out, day before yester."

"And did that telegraph require a trip to my cabin?" *Barney crosses his arms, a defiant pose that leaves a bitter taste in Tanner's mouth. He wants to get off his horse, storm over there, and slap the man for even suggesting noncompliance.* "I done did what I had to, what was agreed upon, and that is that. I sent them on the faraway trail, toward dinosaur alley, just like I said in my message. If the monsters there don't get 'em, you boys sure will. Ain't that right?"

"Oh, it's right," *Tanner says, chewing. Constantly chewing. Chewing like he has the man between his teeth and he's trying to break every one of his bones.* "But the boss requires your presence. Down near *Pteranodon Canyon. We got work for you, and since your loyalty has been proven time and time again, since you're such a good watchdoggy...he wants to promote you to the next level.*"

"Well, tell him to cram it and scram it because I'm not coming. I live here, I'm retired, and I want to be left alone. I pay my mystery tax to the man like everyone else. I sold my...I sold those bounty hunters out because I figured it was the right thing to do, and that it would keep me living free out here, keep me from getting in trouble with the Burner Man, but...that's it. That's the only thing I did it for, and now I kindly ask you to leave me alone. Be gone from this place, you and your outlaws. You and your demon folk."

But the outlaws don't leave. Their horses do not budge an inch in any direction.

" 'Fraid I can't do that, partner," Tanner says, as if he really is sorry about the whole thing. He sees that Barney Reeves doesn't buy an ounce of his faux sympathy, and then says, "Gonna need you to take a ride with us. And please don't protest—I'd hate to see you get hurt. Or that beautiful wife of yours."

A cold hatred burns in the old cowboy's eyes.

"Come on, Barney. I've heard of your legends, the way you used to rundown outlaws. Probably got more kills notched in your belt than me or Burner hisself. But those days are long past you, you know that as well as I know that. So please. Don't resist. Makes no sense. There are four of us and one of you. Odds aren't exactly stacked in your favor, no sir. So don't do the dumb thing and make this a big deal."

"I come with you, I'm a dead man, ain't I?" Barney asks, a slight tremble edging its way into his words. "Ain't I?"

"No, sir. I promise you; you play pigeon, you don't get hurt none. I promise every hair on your wife's head remains untouched."

"I don't like you threatening my wife, Tanner. Don't like it one bit."

"Neither do I, cowboy. Neither do I, but your demeanor isn't lending itself for me to be very nice about things, that's all."

Barney swallows. Opens his mouth to speak. Before one word is uttered, a shotgun blast thunders in the air, and a man from Tanner's gang is pitched off his horse, a red, misty burst materializing where he had sat a moment ago.

Tanner's gun is out of its holster and aimed before anyone can assess what's just happened. Another shot rings out, and Tanner real-

izes, instinctively, that he's gone and popped a reactionary shot himself. In the direction where that shotgun had shouted. He follows his own hand cannon, tracing the position of his arm, and looks down the barrel at his target. Marina Reeves stands completely rigid, holding the smoking shotgun, the left side of her face completely blown away, a red, gaping crater existing where there used to be an eye, an ear, flesh and bone. The shotgun slips from her fingers as the onset of death springs forth in her one remaining eye. Then she sways to the side and does not stop until her cold, lifeless body becomes one with the earth.

Barney shouts her name, his eyes feral, every cord in his neck pronounced.

Tanner sighs as he holsters his weapon. "Go get 'em, boys," he tells his gang as he looks to his one fallen comrade, examining his eyes and realizing that it is too late for him—death has come and whisked him away to the lands of some great beyond, a place Tanner thinks they will all see soon enough.

5

DINOSAUR ALLEY * THE SUN EATER * DO YOU LIKE POE?
* GOODBYE HORSES * YOUR FAVORITE CYCLOPS

Charlie checked the map and checked it twice.
Something didn't sit right with him, and he thought it
was about the direction in which they were heading.
According to the trail Barney Reeves marked for them, they were
supposed to be coming up on the heart of the canyon lands, a
stretch of a few miles that led into the place better known as
Pteranodon Canyon. But that didn't match up to what he was
seeing. Instead, he was looking down past a river—Green River,
he thought, though that would mean the map was off by about
ten clicks and how could that be?—blurred reflections of several
towering rock formations showing atop the sedated surface.
Sparse trees were rooted here and there, little bits of grass
growing in a canvas of earth that wasn't exactly made for
growing such greenery. Mostly everything was clay-colored,

though the rock formations were washed with faded strokes of ambient colors, purples and greens. Charlie figured some scientist could explain these peaceful anomalies, but there wasn't one among the three of them, so he didn't dwell on it for too long. What did consume his thoughts was how far off Barney's mapping had been. An inaccuracy of this degree could not have been done by accident, he surmised, which meant Barney had led them here with purpose, and what that purpose was, Charlie hadn't the slightest. But it concerned him. He had either wanted them to come this way so that they could avoid something or run smack into something. Both ideas sat in his stomach about as well as expired goat's milk.

"Well?" asked Finn. It'd been a day since Charlie had seen the man in his birthday suit, talking nonsense as he was climbing down from the dream smoke's lift. Since then, the man had said maybe two or three words total, and Charlie figured that was due to some personal embarrassment more than anything else. "What's the map say?"

"The map says we're heading in a direction we never intended to go," Charlie admitted once he had his final look and assessment of their trajectory. "What the hell was Barney Reeves doing? Why would he send us so far away from our original destination?"

He handed the map to Nellie to see if she could make some sense of it.

"Don't know," she said, inspecting the trail. "Not like Barney to have some ulterior motive. Maybe he's gotten dumb in his old age. Maybe this is all a mistake."

"You trusted him," Charlie snapped back. "You wouldn't have if he'd given you a clue that he wasn't his old self."

"I suppose that's fair."

"And so, he tricked us."

"We don't know that."

"We know we ain't where we're supposed to be." Charlie pointed at the body of water, the serene fluid movements of its course. "That's the Green River, and, according to the map, that's several miles from where we need to be. The path is all wrong."

Nellie dragged her finger across the map, touching several notable landmarks, as if she was putting Charlie's theory to the test. Then she glanced up at him. "I agree."

"Damn it."

"So, what're our options?" Finn asked. "No sense in arguing about what that old cowboy did or didn't do—doesn't much matter now."

"Well, on that matter, I agree with you." Charlie brought out his pipe from his breast pocket and lit a match to it. Smoked some. Relaxed. Repeated until their current situation dulled on his list of worries.

"We're gonna have to cut through Dinosaur Alley," Nellie said with a long, drawn-out sigh.

The men only looked at her, their blank expressions extending the awkward silence.

"It's the most direct route back to where we need to be," she added.

"No, that's a death trap," Finn said. He glanced around their surroundings as if the area held him to some significant memory. "Should have known we were headed this way. Stupid. How did I not notice we were heading right for it?"

"Probably because you're still not grounded yet," Charlie told him. "All right. I fancy myself experienced in the lands of the west but forgive me for never once having ridden through these particular territories. What can we expect?"

It was Finn's turn to drag a sigh. "Well, if it helps paint a picture, they should really call it Carnivore Alley."

"Meat eaters?"

"Oh, yeah. Some of the biggest. Heard someone ran into a *Giganotosaurus* out here, but that was never proven." He shrugged, as if he only half-believed the story himself. "*Allosaurs*, entire nests of them. Raptors, several different species. Closer to the rivers and lakes you might even find a *Spinosaurus.* You ever see a *Spino*?"

Charlie shook his head.

"No, you ain't. Because, if you had, you wouldn't be alive to tell us about it."

"I get it—it's a dangerous place."

"Aye. Odds are we won't make it through the Alley there alive."

"Seems to be the intention of the man who provided us with an alternate route," Charlie said, shooting Nellie a glare.

"I'd have to agree now that we talked it out," Finn noted.

"Well, I know Barney Reeves—he's like a second father to me. He wouldn't do that to us. Especially not me."

Charlie locked onto her eyes. "Maybe you don't know him like you thought you did." He finished his smoke, knocked out the burnt tobacco leaves, and then hoisted himself back up on his saddle. "Like places, time changes people. Not many of us remain the same forever." He paused to reflect on this, taking a swift look at his own past, the events that had shaped him over the years. Almost all of them were blocked by walls of some towering inferno, the results of a terrible train wreck. "Now, let's get going. We have a lotta ground to make up, and I prefer we blitz through this Dinosaur Alley as if Hell itself were on the path behind us."

No one argued.

They rode out toward the horizon, toward the smell of their almost certain demise.

EVERYTHING HAD BEEN GOING SMOOTHLY, the trio riding into the heart of Dinosaur Alley, when Nellie's horse began to pitch a fit. It had veered off their route some, and then stopped completely, neighing, and bucking in protest. She had tried to pet her, calm down the girl some by whispering in her velvety brown ear, utilizing a soothing voice that usually halted this type of behavior, but nothing worked. The horse kept bucking and rising, not trying to dislodge her per se, but not caring about the rider's safety either. Nellie saw the scribbling on the wall and abandoned the saddle, leaping off to the side to avoid getting dumped on her neck.

"Hell's gotten into her?" Finn asked, looking around for a suspect. "For a place famed for having such teeth, haven't seen but a few roaming herds of herbivores."

"Certainly hasn't been the carnivorous experience you painted so vividly, that's for sure," Charlie told him, hopping off his horse. He approached the bucking mare with some patience, whistling as he raised his hands, attempting to smooth the gal's unease. Like Nellie's previous attempt, the actions brought zero results. "She's worked up about something."

"Maybe there's bound to be thunder in the air," Finn said, glancing up at the vast blue empty. Not a storm cloud in sight, so Nellie was sure that wasn't the case. Besides, her horse had never bucked this much before, not even after being spooked by a pack of raptors.

Very little frightened her and she'd seen her fair share of shit situations, the stickiest kind in fact. So, this very out-of-character reaction to this invisible threat raised Nellie's neck hairs.

"Whatever it is, I think we should make haste," Nellie said, unable to hide the terror inside her.

Charlie whistled at the horse again, and then made some deep guttural noise that was more animal than human, but, surprisingly enough, it worked. The horse planted all four hooves down on the earth, kept them there, and then looked straight on at Charlie, almost as if the bounty hunter had hypnotized her to sleep.

"Easy, girl," he said, approaching her with his hands out. He went to her, gently putting his fingers on her velvety nose. "Eaaaaasy now."

"Well, well," said Finn, clearly impressed. "Looks like ol' Charlie Archer can add 'horse whisperer' to his resume."

Charlie ran his fingers down her face, and then kissed her. The horse neighed with something Nellie thought was affection.

"Thank you, Charlie," she said.

"My pleasure." He looked around the immediate area, as if he expected to see something huge and toothy coming their way, some prehistoric giant bounding from behind the tall formations, eyes flashing with murderous hunger. "We best get going. No telling what that was all about or what she thought was coming."

"You think we should continue along the same path?" Nellie asked.

"Only path we got," Finn interjected. "We go anywhere else, we're apt to get eaten or lost, or both."

Charlie seemed to confirm Finn's claim with a nod. "We ride on. That way, the way we all decided, together."

And that was when the sound of thunder shook the earth, spooking not one but all three horses.

The *Giganotosaurus* emerged from around the rock formation and roared, and when it made the noise that sounded unlike anything Finn had ever heard before, a mixture of some ancient war horn and rolling thunder, the horses took off like the hounds of Hell had been released, and the soul-thirsty bastards were hot on their hooves. Finn's horse darted so quickly that he was thrown off balance, and, when he realized he couldn't correct himself, he ditched the saddle and tumbled to the pathway. He protected his body by tucking himself into a ball and allowing his backside to take the brunt of the impact. Then he continued to roll, as far as he could, until he felt the branches of a small tree stabbing him.

He glanced up immediately and saw that Nellie and Charlie's horses had taken off down the path, following after his gelding. That left them without an exit, and now that the *Giganotosaurus* had emerged onto the scene—still a considerable distance away but any visual of a predator that size was already *too* close—they needed to do one of two things: hunker down somewhere and stay hidden amongst a patch of leafy foliage or run as fast as their legs could carry them. *Giganotosaurus* was slow, nowhere near as fast as its cousin, the *T. rex*, and though Finn had never actually tangoed with one during his adventures, he wouldn't place a bet that the three of them could outrun the monster.

"*Psst*," he said to them. They were clearly captivated by the presence of the enormous fiend, and it took a second call to distract them. "*Let's go.*"

With every step, the dinosaur rattled the earth. Finn felt the tremor move through his body, humming against every organ.

Charlie and Nellie quickly turned away as the *Giganotosaurus* swung its massive, neckless head in their direction, as if it was sweeping the landscape for food. Finn was fairly certain if they stayed hidden that the monster would pass them, but he couldn't be sure. If they had been *rexes,* he'd have found a mud-hole to lie in and cover himself up with the musty scent of wet earth. But he didn't know the first thing about *Giganotosaurus* and its ability to track prey, or if it was even a hunter like the *Tyrannosaur* could be, given the right circumstance and the level of hunger in its belly.

Charlie and Nellie made it over, and Finn watched the carni-vore to see if it took notice. He didn't think so, as the animal gave no clues of an intended pursuit. Instead, the carnivore froze, spying the landscape as if it sensed something there, sensed something hiding. The beast took one enormous step toward them, and Finn felt his scrotum constrict. There was no way it could see them from this distance. Carnivores this huge weren't known for their eyesight. Instead, they relied on their other senses to help seek out their potential kills. Finn flashed his palm at Charlie and Nellie, telling them to keep low and quiet, ride this thing out.

The *Giganotosaurus* pointed its snout in the air and drew in short, noisy breaths, as if the human stink had permeated the entire area. Finn prayed they didn't stink much. There was no mud around to lie down in.

"We should go," Nellie urged, and she was met with a finger over Finn's lips. He didn't know how crazy his eyes went in that moment, but he imagined they looked pretty wild from Nellie's view. Noise was one thing that could doom them in this situation, and even the slightest whisper could attract the ears of this gargantuan predator.

The *Giganotosaurus* listened, swinging its head toward the sound. Stayed there a moment, and to Finn, that moment felt like hours. Through the leaves he watched the dinosaur, examined the way it hunted and marveled over the process. It *knew* they were there. Somewhere. Lurking about. The way a farmer knows he has rabbits in the garden, extensive warrens in the fields. The *Giganotosaurus* sensed food nearby, but it didn't seem ravenous enough to pursue the hunt any further. Another moment of searching the immediate area and the beast lumbered off, farther into the valley, and, eventually, out of sight.

Finn breathed as if it had been a day since his last intake.

The Natives he knew called *Giganotosaurus* "The Sun Eater," and now he knew why.

AN HOUR into the new trail and Charlie's nerves were starting to unravel. They'd lost their horses when the massive carnivore had come rolling through the valley and there were no signs of the three animals. Finn did his best to track their hoofprints, but that only got them so far, and when the dirt and sand turned to grass and taller grass, he'd lost track of them altogether. Luckily, Charlie had kept the map in his back pocket, but his compass, ammo, and snacks—along with various other supplies—were all lost with the horses. He was about to give up hope when Finn told them to get down again.

"What is it now?" Charlie whispered, and Finn immediately shushed him.

They crouched behind some ferns at the base of some tall redwoods. Looking through the leaves, he saw an animal poke its head through some foliage about a hundred feet across the way. When he saw that it was a *Stegosaur,* an infant for that matter, his nerves instantly settled. He almost stood up and walked over to pet the damn thing, but Finn must have sensed that act of kindness coming and placed a hand on his shoulder to keep him crouched.

"Smell that?" Finn whispered in about the lowest tone a man could whisper in.

Considering his sense of smell had dulled some over the years—probably because of the smoking habit—he wasn't surprised to find that he could smell nothing.

"Blood," Nellie said quietly. She faced the men, worry in her eyes. "Lots of it."

When the infant *Stegosaur* moseyed its way out of the bushes, the group could see its body was slicked with fresh red. The scarlet dripped off her and though they could see no visible damage to the herbivore, they knew it had been attacked. Or, at the very least, its herd had been attacked. Somehow, this little feller had escaped.

Charlie fought the urge to run to it. It was the look in the animal's eyes that made him want to, like a motherless kid who had just watched his father die in a lopsided gunfight. Got him thinking of Davey Hill all over again. The *Stego* could barely walk, took only short, pained shuffles forward, and, as it got nearer, Charlie could see the blood along its body did not solely belong to the infant. He couldn't see any visible damage to the body at all. No trenches carved into its flesh, no bite marks. Nothing that suggested the animal was harmed in anyway, at least, not physically. Mentally was another matter, and the post-trauma of whatever had happened was evident in the *Stego's* vacant gaze.

"This isn't good," Finn said. "Let's go."

"We should help it," Charlie said. "It's hurt."

"Are you insane?" Finn pointed to the trees that stood behind the injured infant. "Whatever that *Stego* escaped from will soon find its way here, and we better be gone. What you gonna do for it, besides put it out of its misery?"

"Well, there is that."

"You might need that bullet, mister."

Finn was right about that. Now that their supply was missing, they didn't need to go around wasting what they had on their persons.

"All right," Charlie said, succumbing to the notion that Finn was right, and hating that that was so. "Lead the way."

But before he could, something roared.

Something big, something with teeth.

WHEN THE *GIGANOTOSAUR* ripped through the branches, knocking over trees like empty beer glasses caught in the storm of some drunkard's rage, Nellie's heart nearly stopped dead. In a blink, the thing's shadow fell over the tiny *Stego,* a dark blanket of doom. And the *Stego* knew it too. Its eyes shot open with a primal fear she'd never seen in any living creature that was about to die. Untamed terror flashed before her, and, as the enormous mouth closed around the infant's body, Nellie closed her eyes, unable to watch the swift execution. She heard the crunching of bones, the squelching of hot blood through opened flesh. The colossal creature's satisfied grunts, along with the subsequent roar of victory, the thunderous noise shaking loose branches from the trees, sending twittering birds from their nests, into the endless sky above.

As the dinosaur feasted on its kill, Nellie felt someone tapping on her shoulder. It was Finn, and he was telling her to move along, that it was time to go. Enough lingering. Now was the best time to safely make their exit. The infant offered a limited amount of meat, and the beast would finish its meal in almost no time at all.

Nellie followed him through the brush, making sure each footstep was a near-silent one, and that there were no divots in the landscape that would trip her up, cause her to slip and fall. They operated in stealth until that gruesome scene was well behind them.

And then they searched for a way out of the woods, and, somehow, a way into *Pteranodon Canyon*.

"WE'RE LOST, JUST ADMIT IT," Finn said about an hour's walk away from the spot where the infant *Stego* had met its brutal end. "I don't know why you won't just admit it."

Charlie clenched his jaw, trying his best to keep what was on his mind from reaching his lips. "We're not lost, all right. I have a good idea where we're headed, and that's this way."

This way was through a small narrow path barely wide enough for one human. The forest had edged them out and was closing in on them. Soon, no path would exist at all, just walls of branches and foliage, too much for them to climb through. Not to mention, who knew what disease-carrying insects or poisonous snakes were living in these areas. Charlie certainly didn't—he had no idea at all. Just that this was the way they were headed before the *Gigano-whatever-it-was-called* came and mucked things up for them.

"Charlie," Nellie said, trying to play the role of mediator. "Why don't we settle down and try to figure out our next move."

"Because our next move is this way." He continued to take the path, pushing branches away from his face, making sure they didn't snap back and hit the person behind him, which happened to be Nellie. Finn, he didn't much care whether the branches took a swipe at him or not; in fact, he kinda wished they would. "It'll be dark soon and we have no supplies. Did you forget our horses decided to up and leave us?"

"I haven't forgotten," she said, her voice holding an optimistic tone. She was a little too arrogant in her own way, but Charlie appreciated her honesty, her refreshing candor. Finn on the other hand...well, he wished the man would keep his mouth shut for the rest of their journey. He didn't add much to their trip save a little turmoil. "But at this rate, I think we can safely assume that—"

"What?" he asked, spinning on her. "What? That we're lost? That we don't know where we're going? That we're in the middle of a fucking place called Dinosaur Alley and we have no idea how to get out?"

"Yes, Charlie. That."

"Well, remember whose map it was that put us here."

She bit back her words; he could see it in the way her cheeks flexed. "I remember. And I cannot express how sorry I am that my decision led us here, no matter what the cause of this unfortunate predicament truly is."

"Truth is, you trusted someone you shouldn't-a. And now we're heading toward our own deaths." He shook his head. "Should have ridden this one out alone. Should-a never agreed to any of this."

"Charlie," she said, as if hurt by this particular dig.

"Y'all want to stay put, 'figure out' your next move? Fine. Go ahead. I ain't stopping ya." With that, he turned, heading back into the brush, disappearing behind the green folds and leafy extensions with zero hesitation in his steps. He didn't turn around, didn't even think about doing so. Thought hadn't crossed his mind, and any time he thought it might, he thought about something else—the bluest sky, the greenest valley, the yellowest mountains. Purple mornings and gray afternoons. The colors of life kept all other thoughts away.

"Let him go," he heard Finn say.

And so, he did.

He went. By himself. Further into the lost jungle of Dinosaur Alley.

"STUPID," Finn said, once he was sure Charlie was good and out there, a place where he could speak freely without raising the man's ire. "Stupid, stubborn bastard, he is. Don't worry about him. He's a dumb old cowboy who thinks he knows it all, and he ain't ever gonna change, so don't even bother with him or anyone like him."

Nellie stood there and watched the spot where Charlie had disappeared.

Finn approached her from behind, gentle steps. "Come on, Nell. Let's go. Let's double back where we were before we got lost, before the *Giganotosaurus* threw us off the trail. We can get there before dark and hunker down, grab a nap, and hopefully wake up tomorrow without a raptor harvesting our bodies for parts. Yeah? How's that sound?"

"We shouldn't separate."

"He chose his path."

"It's not right."

"Look, we all want the same thing, right?" He raised his hands as if the whole world wanted the same thing and not just their trio. "But we all have different ideas on how to obtain it. We needed a leader, and Charlie Archer—he was about the closest thing we had to one, and, well, I don't know much about leading, haven't done it ever in my life, but that—that is not how you lead. You do not walk out on your gang. A shepherd doesn't leave his sheeps."

"It's just sheep."

"What?"

"Plural of sheep is still sheep."

"Whatever."

"He was right. It was my fault." She hung her head, and he could see tears springing forth from her eyes. "I trusted Reeves —he was like a father to me, Finn. Like a father. Maybe even treated me better than my own father, and he fucking sent us this way, to this goddamn death trap?"

"Hey," he said, getting nearer, testing the proximity by holding out his hands, as if there was a chance she would reject his touch and he wanted to be certain before he committed to any act of said touching. "Hey, come 'ere." Putting his arms around her, he pulled her close, burying his nose in her hair, the smell of it. Didn't smell great—like river water that clung to the threads of old clothing—but it was hers and he was close to it, which wasn't all that bad in his opinion. "We can still do this. Together. You and me."

She moved in a way that put their lips closer. He didn't move at all. Couldn't. He was powerless to this new emotion that swept through him, this thing that burned in the center of his chest. Then their lips met. Their pairing was quick, and then the separation that followed was even quicker.

"No," she said, though, in Finn's opinion, she was the one

who had started it. Well, maybe not, he thought, but she had surely allowed it to happen, and that was as good as starting it from where Finn Hampton was standing. "No, we can't become distracted."

"Maybe a good distracting is what we need."

She ignored this advice and returned to her view of the deserted woods, where Charlie Archer had departed with seemingly no intention of coming back. Finn grew to hate Charlie in that moment, hated his guts for a few reasons—chief among them being that his attitude and departure dampened the mood of the early evening, thus putting Nellie in a foul mood, one not suitable for kissing. And the stuff that could come after the kissing.

"Maybe he'll come back," Finn suggested, one last attempt to reel her in.

"No," she said, "I don't think we'll ever see Charlie Archer again." Then she swung her head back to him, a distant terror injected into her eyes. "At least...not alive."

IT WASN'T LIKE him to get so pissed off like that. He was a mild-mannered man by most standards, always had been. He couldn't help it; that was just the way he was raised. But something about the whole situation had driven him over the edge, and he thought—now that he had some time away from it—he couldn't really pinpoint what that something was and why it had irked him so.

He came to a clearing just beyond where, spectacularly, the path opened wide, allowing for an easy walk in the jungle-like forest. In the clearing stood men and horses, too many to count at first. After the initial shock of seeing others and being fulfilled with a new hope, he took a mental step back and counted up the men and horses, plus the three extras that had no riders atop them. Nine horses, six men, each of them coarse and rugged as far as men go. More dirt and grime brushed their flesh than didn't, and Charlie could tell they'd been on the trail for a good week, maybe more. A bathhouse was what they needed, but out here, in Dinosaur Alley, there was no such thing.

But it wasn't the men that kept Charlie's attention. It was the horses, the extras. *Their* horses. Charlie's, Nellie's, and Finn's. The animals were unharmed, looking as sedated as they had been back at Oat Creek. The men who had found them had taken great care in settling their nerves, though the men themselves did not look like beacons of kindness. They looked like ruffians of the diabolical sort, men whose intentions were less than benevolent.

They looked like outlaws.

"Well, hey there, friend," said one of them, the one who was holding Charlie's horse by his lead. He wore a black hat, a black shirt, and black patch over one eye. "Lose some horses?"

"Aye, lost a few, yeah," Charlie said, ambling his way across the clearing, toward his new *friends*. He approached each step with caution, making sure to keep his hands a considerable distance from the revolvers on each hip, fearing that he would seem too trigger-happy, too eager to turn this situation into a violent forum. But he didn't let his guard down either. Instead, he kept his hands within a safe, comfortable span, so that if he needed his guns to join the conversation, he was ready. "Can't thank you enough for reining them in. Much praise to you, gentlemen. If I had a few coins, I'd surely toss them your way to compensate for the bother."

"No bother at all," Eye-Patch said, waving a limp wrist. "We was just cruising through and saw these beauties all by them lonesome. Saw that they were saddled up, so...knew they had to be belonging to somebody."

"Well, I thank you regardless." Charlie stopped a few feet in front of the man and his crew, Eye-Patch clearly squatting on the role of leader, as no one else dared to contribute to their dialogue, nor did they look like they wanted to. He half-expected the man to hand over the leads, but, when he didn't, Charlie was also not surprised.

He wants something, Charlie thought, trying to see through the man's intentions, trying to find out what was actually happening here before it was too late. Before Charlie ended up the victim of some trail robbery, left to die in the jungle, left for the wandering scavengers of Dinosaur Alley. But they didn't want money. No, if they had, they would have helped themselves to the saddlebags and been on their way. No, it was something else. And the longer the seconds passed in silence, the more Charlie began to think this meeting was not one of coincidental mishap.

Then he pieced it together.

Billy-Boy Tanner.

The photograph Smitty had shown them back at the Oyster was suddenly recalled, the eye-patch triggering the memory.

"I'm gonna cut straight through the bullshit, if it pleases you," Tanner said, some semblance of a grin crossing his face, the restrained sort. "I've had a look at your effects and...well, if

I'm being honest, we knew you were coming down the trail this way, had us a little inside information coming down the chain."

Charlie kept up his stony appearance, not giving anything away. "Figured you might have. Tanner, right?"

"My reputation precedes me."

"Indeed. Something to be proud of, I'm sure."

Tanner took this as the insult it was. "You know, I could kill you right here and now, no one on Earth would come looking for you."

"That I believe."

"But Burner...man, does he want a reunion with you. Must have had some lasting effect on him. Never seen the mention of another man get under his skin, like."

"I've been known to make an impression on folks."

"Wouldn't have guessed it from our brief talk. But...never judge a book by the first few pages, right?"

"Never took you for the reading sort."

"I'm well-read, Mr. Archer. You ever read Poe?"

"Not a big fan of him myself," Charlie said. "Was always more of a Hawthorne guy."

"Well, Poe is my weakness. His stories just get to me, you know. I love the dread they inspire. 'Specially that one about the heart. You read it?"

"I read it," Charlie said, amused at the conversation he was having with this renegade outlaw. A literary discussion of all things. "Surprised you could read it, having one eyeball and all." This didn't seem to sting the man as much as he had intended.

"Well, I surely don't read as fast as I used to," he said with a gruff laugh that sounded like newspaper being crumpled between angry hands. "But that tale about the heart underneath the floorboards. Damn, runs my blood cold every time."

Charlie had humored the man long enough. He kept a smile

present, but inside he was burning. "I'm sure we have more important matters to discuss, sir. Like, my effects, Francis Burner, those horses there—"

Tanner pulled out his revolver and shot Charlie's horse directly in the face. Blood exploded like a stick of dynamite, and Charlie recoiled from the sudden burst of violence. The other two horses protested the plain murder by hopping away from the scene of the crime, but Tanner's men corralled them with ease, stopped them from shuffling more than a few feet.

His gelding lay in the dirt, blood trickling from the head hole, a splash of brains resting beside him. Charlie could see his saddlebag had been purged.

"That brought me no pleasure, Mr. Archer," Tanner said, and there indeed was no gleeful expression on the outlaw's face. "But we need to get down to business. No more shit. Understand?"

Charlie's mouth was almost too dry to answer. "Yes," he croaked.

"Good. Now. Francis Burner wants you alive, but he said nothing about your two friends. Although, we cut a sweet deal with the Negro cowboy and part of that deal is to leave the lady alive." He looked to his boys, that evil grin testing the elasticity of his cheeks. "Though, the nature of her condition upon leaving her alive is up for interpretation, as far as I'm concerned." His focus was on Charlie again, sharpening that harsh glare. "But it's that boy I want. Truly. Him and I—we got a business to settle."

"Boy?"

"Goes by the name of Finn Hampton, though I've known him as another. Name was Denny Gerhardt when he came into my employment, just a few years back."

"Finn..."

"Finn. Son of a devil, that one. Surprised a prestigious bounty hunter like yourself associates with such degeneracy."

Charlie scanned the man's one good eye, as if the truth were hidden just behind the hazy-red sclera. "Finn—what'd he do?"

"Him?" Tanner's hand went to his eye patch, lifting it up, revealing the cavernous indent of wrinkled, dead flesh, a scar over the sense that was. "That son of a bitch turned me cyclopean."

Dark settled on Dinosaur Alley. It was a cold dark, the kind that made Nellie wish she had some blankets to keep warm. If not blankets, at least an extra layer of clothing. A wool sweater or a bear-hide jacket. Hell, with this particular autumnal freeze, she would have given a finger for a couple bundles of newspaper to stuff her current attire.

"Cold?" Finn asked, though he had to see the way she sat close to the fire, rubbing her shoulders.

"What gave it away?"

"You know, body warmth can really—"

"I'm gonna shut you down right there, Mr. Hampton."

"Oh...I'm Mr. Hampton now?"

"You've always been Mr. Hampton."

"But, before, when we were—"

"I don't know what happened before, but I'd like it if we both forgot what happened and moved on from it."

"Nell, we had—"

"We had nothing, Hampton." *No "mister" this time, perfect,* she thought. *That'll bother him even more.* "Nothing. Hear me? Got caught up in the moment, is all. I'd rather not think about it, as I said, and furthermore, you got anything to wash your taste out of my mouth, give it here."

Finn hung his head. "Alright. Well, that's that, I suppose."

"That's that."

"Guess I'll tuck in for the night. You got first watch?"

She swallowed the dryness down. "Yes."

"Perfect."

"Fine."

"Wake me up in two hours. All I need to get me through the rest of the way, provided we can find it and don't get attacked before that."

"Two hours it is."

With that, he shuffled off to the makeshift bed of gathered leaves.

She watched the fire crackle, closed her eyes, and wished she was home, sitting next to the stove, her father, a healthy version of the man who had raised her, telling her stories of the glory days of the Old West, when the frontier was young and unexplored, just like he had when she was a kid, when things were simple.

THEY PACKED UP—THOUGH there wasn't much to pack—and headed out at first light, under the tangerine skies of Dinosaur Alley. They doubled back to where they'd first gotten lost and proceeded to follow their original route, taking the trail up around the mountain range, bypassing the thick jungle of this terrible territory. At least here, out in the open, they could see the danger coming. In the jungle, they had no chance of protecting themselves on foot.

After a climb up some rocks, they were forced to head back into the jungle simply because there was no other place to go, which made Finn especially nervous knowing what he knew about the area and its notorious reputation for killing cowboys and merchant wayfarers. So, having to head back in did not please him in the slightest, but it was either that or climb back down, double back, and start over again. Which they both decided they would not do.

They walked along the jungle path, which was easy enough to travel down and not as overrun with splendid vegetation as their previous path, until they came to a clearing. In the center of the clearing were three horses, all of them dead, with bullet holes in their heads. Brains splattered around the forest's floor, resting and gelled up like dropped jars of jam. They recognized the three bodies at once, even though a roving pack of *Hesperonychus* had dug into the meaty centers of them, picked away at most of the muscle and fat, leaving behind nothing but the bones. A few of the chicken-like dinosaurs, no bigger than a house cat, were still pilfering what they could, a couple of them buried so far into the bodily tunnels that the horseflesh pulsated like worms writhing just below a soft, earthy surface.

"Git!" Finn said, stomping over to the kill site. The *Hesperonychus* ditched their efforts and made for the trees, fleeing like mice caught with their noses in a wheel of cheese. Once the area had been cleared of the tiny buggers, Finn dropped to one knee beside the fallen horses and examined what had actually killed them. "Horses been shot."

Nellie looked on, surveying the damage on her own.

"Fuck," Finn muttered, standing up, weak knees barely able to support his wobbly upper half. He felt sick, the sudden illness turning the world slightly gray, and spinning the way he used to when playing that old child's game, the one where he and friends spun themselves in circles and then competed by seeing who could walk the farthest with an unbalanced equilibrium. It was like the end of those games, when his senses were returning to normal. "Who the fuck was out here shooting our horses?" It wasn't a question he expected Nellie to answer, but the woman bent down and picked up a piece of paper, a note, that had been stuffed in one of the horse's unmoving ears. "What's that?"

She unfolded the letter, allowed her eyes to digest the words before them. Couldn't have been a long one, seeing how short the paper was, but she sure took her damn time reading it, unless she was reading it three, four times over just to make sure she understood every word.

"What is it?" he asked, watching her turn whiter than her usual complexion. "Just what the hell is it?"

She walked over to him and handed him the note. His eyes immediately scanned the page:

DEAR FINN,

I HAVE YOUR PAL, CHARLIE ARCHER, AND ME AND HIM ARE GONNA HEAD TO PTERANODON CANYON AND WAIT UNTIL YOU GET THERE, SO WE CAN SORT OUT THIS MESS. SEE YOU SOON, OLD BUDDY.

BEST,

YOUR FAVORITE CYCLOPS,

BBT

FINN DROPPED the note on the ground, not realizing he was gritting his teeth so hard until he heard something snap in his jaw. Probably just a muscle pulling and not a broken tooth, but he couldn't be sure because everything from his neck up had gone a little numb. He supposed that was on account of the adrenaline flooding his system. He glanced up at Nellie, who looked none too pleased about the letter that had been left behind and—probably—that the element of surprise had now been stolen from them. That was practically all they had in their favor heading into *Pteranodon* Canyon, knowing they'd be up against at least three, four dozen outlaws, all armed to the teeth with shooters that shot straighter than anything they could have purchased over the counter back in Oat Creek. But...if they were destined to fall in *Pteranodon* Canyon, then so be it as far as Finn Hampton was concerned. He'd felt awful about how the trip had gone, how he'd messed things up and made the journey a lot harder on everyone, and now, he owed it to Charlie Archer to finish the job or die trying.

"Can you track them to *Pteranodon* Canyon?" asked Nellie.

Finn examined the horseshoe impressions in the dirt. "Yeah," he said, then looked back to his dead gelding. "But we might not need to."

He dug his fingers into the horse's ear, and from it he

extracted another folded piece of paper. It was a map. Drawn by Billy-Boy Tanner himself.

Finn's favorite cyclops.

SHOWDOWN AT PTERANODON CANYON

When Charlie Archer opened his eyes, he was not where he should have been. He expected to see grand canyons and skies filled with prehistoric birds, the powerful sun's descending rays filling his eyes and warming the exposed flesh of his arms and face. But instead, he found himself in a grassy field, looking up at ashen clouds that huddled together, concealing the sun from reaching this gloomy morning. He smelled smoke. Lots of it. In fact, that terrible smoke was so pungent he could even see it—it was the tumultuous black kind, the type that unfurled with a potent rage. And when he looked to the north, that was exactly what he saw. Smoke. The blackest kind, roiling up from a lively fire that was built on a bed of charcoal beginnings. And those beginnings belonged to a passenger's cabin.

He knew where he was before the scenery could fully reveal itself. He had traveled back to that day, and had done so under his own power, without the help of dream smoke or peyote or some other hallucinatory ingestible. He was here, and here now.

Pushing himself to his feet, he was extremely impressed with how authentic everything appeared, how his senses responded to this incorporeal world. He could smell that heavy wet fog, that musty odor that clung to the air, underneath the smoke that attempted to dominate everything. The grass had felt springy on his palms when he pushed himself up. The sounds of people screaming found his ears, and their terror was genuine.

Just as it had been on that day.

"Rose..." he thought, and then started running. As he sprinted toward the train and the fireballs exploding from the middle cars, he wondered if this *was* real. If he had actually traveled back to this point in time and everything he'd experienced after, those hard years of living without his family, was nothing but a savage dream. A nightmare, a punishment for some bad thing he'd done in his life, and though he could recall none that would warrant such torture, he was sure there was something he'd done to earn him a trip to Hell in the Lord's eyes. "Rose," he said again, more frantically as he began to put more stock in this notion that everything before him was reality. That everything else he'd come to know was a terrible lie.

He got to the fire, about twenty yards from the mounting flames, and saw people trying to escape the car through the open windows. He didn't see Rose, didn't see Trevor, his only son's cute, smiling face, the one he'd kissed the forehead of every night he was home for the first five years of the youngster's life. The climbers were engulfed in flames, the fiery embers dancing in the air like the floating eyes of some medieval dragon, and the climbers were falling out, onto the ground, seeking safety from the crash. They were rolling in the wet grass of the gray morning, but this was no use. They were already as good as dead, already burning their way to a black death.

He cupped his hands around his mouth and shouted, "ROSE!"

There were no answers, and the screams only intensified. Grew louder at his request for his wife to answer.

Then, the car exploded, the flames and whatever chemicals were trapped there reaching their corrosive end. Shrapnel and body parts were sent outward in an impressive boom, causing Charlie to cower from the incoming projectiles. He hit the ground and covered his head as parts of train and parts of people came showering down around him. When he finally mustered the guts to look up, he saw a severed arm sitting next to a compass, a detached leg resting next to the cabin's grab bar. Those who did not die in that particular explosion crawled away from the fiery wreckage, screaming as they lazily tried to scoop their guts back into their opened abdomens or frantically tried to reattach an arm or leg, as if the surgery was going to somehow magically conduct itself without any of the necessary tools and stitching. The already-dead people were sobbing because they knew they had reached the end of the line on this railroad called *Life*. Their train had derailed because of the madman outlaw Francis Burner, and they would die in this open field.

This was not reality, Charlie tried to tell himself. This had happened years ago and now, for some reason, he was witnessing the horror again.

Somewhere beyond the smoke was a shadowed devil with red eyes. He watched from atop the hill as the wrecked train burned, fires consuming every inch of steel. Charlie locked onto the shadow's gaze, and then realized it wasn't shadows that covered the figure's body, but soot. It was a survivor.

It was Francis Burner.

He was alive, and, in that moment, Charlie realized he'd known it all along. That Burner had somehow survived while everyone else on that train had died—railroad workers, passengers, and heist-men in Burner's employ.

Francis Burner had survived, and you knew that, didn't you? He tormented himself with this knowledge. *You knew that but you convinced yourself he was dead because that made it easier to deal*

*with, made it easier knowing that he killed your family, the only
people you ever truly cared about. Made it easier to live your life.*

*Francis Burner was alive this whole time, and you could have
gone after him, killed him, got revenge for slaying your wife and kid.*

But you didn't. Cause you're too chicken-shit.

Not the man everyone thinks you are.

No, he thought back, *no, I didn't know he survived.*

But he couldn't be certain. A part of him thought the play-
back was nothing but truth, a truth he had buried deep in his
own soul, one he planned to never dig up, not on his darkest
day.

Now that it had been unearthed, he had no reason to
reject it.

He knew, all right. Knew that Burner was alive, and he chose
to ignore it, go searching for him because the whole country
thought Burner had died in that wreck. So why fight popular
opinion. Burner was as good as dead anyway—no way he'd ever
rear his ugly head again. So, he had convinced himself that it
was a vision, just a reaper he'd seen on that hill, watching over
all the souls it'd come to harvest, and not Francis Burner
himself.

Lies he told himself to keep on living.

That's all it ever was.

Lies.

But lies buried in oneself were always dug up, and now
Charlie Archer knew the truth, and knew what had to be done
—he had to kill Francis Burner once and for all.

He had to.

WHEN HE WOKE up for the second time, he found himself in a cage, naked, alone, and feeling quite cold. He was in the dark mostly, a small tunnel of light beaming toward him. The air had a wet quality, the damp-earth scent rising above the faint tinge of blood. After surveying his body, he discovered some of his flesh was missing, strips here and there that had been lashed away. His nose ran bloody, the irony taste standing bold on the tip of his tongue.

Charlie was in bad shape, and he knew it.

His legs weren't strong enough to stand, so he didn't even attempt it. There was nowhere to go anyway. The cage they'd put him in looked well-built, and the odds of them making a faulty unit for him to break out of weren't that great. Maybe he'd attempt to escape when some of his strength returned, after they fed him and gave him water.

If they did.

Maybe they were attempting to starve him, about the cruelest way you could see a man out of this world.

Charlie couldn't (for the life of him) figure out why he was still alive. There was no need for it, not really. If Burner wanted him kept alive, it had to be for his own personal satisfaction, and maybe Burner wanted to personally end this rivalry that had been going on damn-near a decade. Either way, Charlie wasn't thankful. A large part of him wanted to be dead, wanted his soul to drift toward the big sky, where Rose and Trevor Archer were waiting for him, beyond those pearly gates where the angels waited to greet him with open arms. Death was his number one choice, and every other outcome was a far second.

About an hour after he came to light, he heard footsteps brushing against the caverns sandy ground, the approaching figure a foot-dragger if he had ever heard one. It was like he was lugging something heavy behind him and couldn't pick up his feet. When the figure stepped into the frail light the staked torches provided, he saw a man he did not recognize, not even from Tanner's gang who'd brought him here. But clearly he was a villain, done up in classic outlaw attire, and he even had a red bandana that covered the lower half of his face, as if he were robbing a bank in these canyon lands and didn't want anyone catching the slightest glimpse of him in order to avoid the lawmen getting a decent sketch of the perpetrator. The man had a tray of food—eggs and some smoked meat. Charlie didn't know why but it seemed like too decent a meal for a prisoner.

"Gonna open this up," Red-Bandana said, crouching by the cage, near the door Charlie hadn't noticed as it had blended in with the rest of the bamboo bars. "You make a move for me and I'll have a bullet in you faster than you can say 'Stegosaurus salad.' Got me, friend-o?"

Charlie nodded in agreement, because even if he had wanted to, there was no play to make an escape. Even if he over-powered this man, and stole his gun, there were probably twenty or thirty more right outside waiting to put him down.

Though, again, that was what he sort of wanted. To go out in this blaze of glory, taking out as many of Burner's men as possible before his body was fed the lead. But he was too weak. And even though the lure of death was somewhat attractive, there was a part of him that knew his dead wife would be somehow disappointed in him for giving up so easily. Rose, had she been alive today, would slap him for wanting such a thing.

He could almost hear her scolding him. Telling him to sack up, that the time for dying wasn't now, that death was far worse than anything he could possibly imagine, that living was a gift, something to cling to. Life was hope, and he should not shun hope in any form it assumed.

Keep on living, Charlie Archer, he heard her say. *You keep on living now, and don't you worry none about me and yours. We're okay.*

And so, as Red-Bandana left behind the tray of eggs and sliced meats, as he ate from the gift, he decided he would live. He would fight. Or, at least, he would die trying to breathe one last breath.

WALKING their way out of Dinosaur Alley was not a pleasant journey, but they managed. Several times they were forced to hunker down and hide from their enemies, roving packs of carnivores and giant predators that stalked the jungle lands of western Wyoming. Finn was surprised they were able to dodge the carnivores as easily as they had. An *Allosaurus* had almost discovered their scent as they crouched down in a blackberry bush. Finn had instructed Nellie to crush the berries and rub the juices across her face, and he demonstrated this tactic by doing the exact same thing. She had followed suit and rubbed her face and arms in the dark juices that ran from the crushed berries, and the dinosaur had gotten so close to discovering them that Finn had almost relieved himself in his britches. Though he managed to keep his bladder full during the ordeal, it had been one of his closest brushes with death-by-dinosaur. The *Allosaurus* had sniffed the air between them, the hedge of bushes the only thing separating the humans from the massive predator's hungry teeth, and it had somehow passed on the opportunity to further explore the strange scent it was picking up from beyond the rows of blackberry bushes. It had moved on, much to Finn's delight.

Hours later, they washed off the berry juice in a river. What was repellent for some was alluring for others, and they didn't need to attract further attention to themselves than two humans strolling through a dinosaur-infested jungle already had.

There had been other close calls but none that warranted a gunfight. Once out of the alley and back on the main trail, the pair followed the map Tanner had sketched for them, heading toward the giant X with the label "*Pteranodon* Canyon" written in perfect cursive.

About six hours later, they had made it to the outskirts of Tanner's camp. Or Burner's camp. Finn didn't know who was truly in charge of this operation, and he wouldn't have put it past Tanner to reinvent Francis Burner and use a ghost story as subterfuge for his operation. Francis Burner being alive would make a perfect cover story for the truth, that Tanner was really in charge of things out here, and that would draw the eyes of the law away from him, Tanner's specialty. He always had been good at dodging Johnny Law. Little mind tricks and ruses were what made Tanner so elusive, and this "Francis Burner rising from beyond the grave" was the perfect cover story to drape over himself.

They reached the canyon lands and made camp on the outskirts, far enough from Tanner's camp so their firelight wouldn't attract any unwanted attention. Finn made sure to keep the fire low as to not risk the possibility of such a thing.

"What's the plan?" asked Nellie, and she was right—they hadn't discussed what they were going to do once they got here. Finn had been putting it off in hopes that Nellie was going to come up with something. "You do have a plan, don't you?"

"Was hoping you'd have something for us."

"Since when do you care what my opinion is?"

He rolled his eyes. She sure was a fiery one, and that, he thought, was what made her so damn attractive. "Look, Nell, you're the bounty hunter here, I'm just—" He stopped himself. What was he going to say? What was he going to say that was truthful? What was he exactly? Did he even know the answer himself? "I'm just a criminal."

She stared at him like the information didn't surprise her.

"There, I said it."

She continued to eye him, the admission seeming to mean nothing to her, information that was already received and processed in her noggin prior to him saying so. "You may be, but that makes you perfect for what comes next."

"You ain't mad?"

"That you're a criminal?" She shook her head. "No, I figured as much when you said you once threw in with a man like Billy-Boy Tanner."

Finn warmed his hands near the fire. "Look, I'm a rotten son-of-a-bitch. But I ain't killed that kid, that's a goddamn promise."

"I believe you."

"Wish Charlie would-a believed me."

"Well, I wouldn't worry about that now." She dragged her finger along the dirt, and, at first, Finn didn't have a clue as to what she was doing. Then, he realized. "We need a distraction."

"Distraction?"

"Something to lure them out."

"What'll that be?"

"I think that can be *you*."

Finn fixed his brow. "The hell're you talking about?"

"Think about it."

He searched his noggin, but he couldn't come up with one good reason why he would (or should) act as the bait in any plotted ruse.

"But you'll need my guns?"

She nodded. "And I'll have them."

He dragged out a sigh like a child told to go to bed early on Christmas Eve. "Well, all right. I guess so. I mean, just the two of us—how much of a shot do we have against thirty-plus men anyways, some of the meanest motherfuckers the west has to offer, all armed with itchy trigger fingers and swollen with bloodlust?"

"Not much of one," she admitted, though her smile suggested she knew something he didn't, and if he was being honest, it was starting to piss him off.

"What's in your head, lady?"

"How well do you know your dinosaurs?" she asked, her eyes smiling, going along with her curling lips.

It was three hours later when the men came to stock the empty cage next to him. Took all of three seconds to figure out who the other naked man was. Barney Reeves, nude as the day his mother had shat him out of the womb, was paraded into the cave and tossed into his small bamboo cell. The old man spilled to the floor rather roughly, and Charlie thought a man his age shouldn't be handled with such carelessness, though he gathered the men who'd captured him didn't give any shits when it came to the aged cowboy's well-being. Charlie figured him being alive was lucky enough.

"Well, well," Charlie said, leaning his head against the bamboo structure. "If it isn't the coward, Barney Reeves."

Barney huddled up into a corner, his eyes shifting back and forth like he expected the shadows behind him to throw punches.

"You got anything to say for yourself?" Charlie asked, expecting no answer. But there was nothing else to do in the cave save for watching the time pass, and that was as much fun as watching field grass grow. "Anything at all?"

Barney didn't respond, but he did shift his eyes in Charlie's direction.

"She trusted you, you know. Like a father. 'More than my *own* father,' I believe were her words."

At this Barney began to tear. It didn't take long for the old man to start sobbing like a mother who had just lost a baby during a turbulent childbirth.

Charlie let him have a good cry, was thankful the outlaws weren't around to see it. After he couldn't stomach the old cowboy weeping any longer, he said, "Quit it now. Don't want them to think they've gone and broken you. Don't credit them for their non-accomplishments."

The man dammed his eyes. "Can't help it. I ain't just crying about that—those wretched bastards...they gone and killed my Marina."

"Well, when you get in league with such creatures of deviant behavior...what'd you expect?"

"Still..." Barney blotted his eyes with a naked wrist. "She was my...well hell, I never known another woman quite like her. Deviant creatures or not, that doesn't make the truth any easier to swallow."

"Well, chew it quickly and quietly then. We have work to do."

"Work?"

Charlie leaned forward, pressing his face against the bamboo bars so the old cowboy could see the fury that had gripped his cheeks. "You want to sit naked in this cage forever, Reeves? Is that it? You givin' up on life now that you fucked the rest of us?"

"Might as well," he said hopelessly. "You see how many of them are out there? We're outmatched by at least sixty hand cannons. And you and I don't even got *one* between the two of us."

"We'll have to shoot our way out with our brains, then."

"Outsmart them?"

"Why the hell not?"

"Because...when it comes to wits versus guns, the guns always win."

Charlie chewed on that for second. "I refuse to lie down and die for Francis Burner."

As if mentioning the man's name summoned him magically, a figure appeared at the end of the cave's only entrance and exit. He smelled like smoke and death, and when he moved toward the cages, his pockets jingled with the riches of dead men.

"I hear my name being mentioned?" the dark figure asked, and when he stepped into the torchlight, Charlie felt a heat rise within himself. "Charlie Archer, the most famous bounty hunter in the west. My, my! How good it is to see you again, Charlie! Enjoying yourself, I see. Passing the time by piddling your diddle, are we?"

Charlie glared at the man who must have been dead, because the color of his flesh was that of a fish that had washed ashore days ago. An expired, bluish-gray.

"Well, how about it, Charlie? Aren't you going to tell me how good it is to see me again? How you've been dreaming about this moment since we said our silent, long goodbyes on that hill, oh-say...seven years was it?"

"Six and seven months," Charlie huffed.

"Six and seven months," Burner repeated. "Six long years and seven long months, I bet. For you. Not me. I've been busy."

"So I've heard."

"Never came looking for me, Charlie. And why is that, exactly? Thought you'd be gunning for me since day one."

"Thought you'd died."

Burner cocked his head back and howled like a coyote stricken with some disease that makes them foam at the teeth. "Ooooooo-weee!" he howled, the wolf-like noise causing the hairs on Charlie's neck to rise. "That's a good one, Charlie, a real good one. But...you saw me. Didn't you? Didn't you see me on the hill as the wreckage burned? I saw *you*. And you did see me, we locked eyes, you and me. Our souls met that night, Charlie Archer. No other way about it."

"Aye," Charlie said, admitting the man was speaking the truth. "I guess I convinced myself that you were a mirage of sorts. That no one could have survived that fire, and so...I just believed you were dead because that notion filled me with comfort and joy. Got me through these last six-plus years, knowing you were dead, burned to ash."

"Must kill you to know otherwise, I reckon."

Charlie nodded. "Doesn't feel too good knowing you're still breathing. That's for sure."

Burner bent forward, keeping his legs straight and stiff as if the top half of his body were pinned to his hips. "You want to know, don't you? How I did it? How I walked through the fire, the flames? How I walked straight through Hell and came out the other side? How Perdition never wrangled good ol' Francis Burner? Bet it's killing you to know."

"I am a mite curious." Charlie surveyed the flesh of Francis's face. Its rather smooth nature perplexed him. He thought it would have been riddled with craters of scars, purpled over with the healing touch strong burns bring the skin. "Guessin' you got some story about pacts with devils or the like."

At this Francis grinned, a purposeful demonic sneer. "Well shit, Charlie. I ain't about to go and tattle on the devil, am I? Course not. Be bad business, that. But..." He turned his eyes to the cave's craggy ceiling, as if asking the heavens permission for whatever came next. "But I can tell you that my business with him is over, and I got new business to leisure in."

"Poaching 'dactyls, I see."

Burner smiled. "That old hog presidenté we got putting the hit out on us, I bet."

"Something like that. There are many parties interested in your revival."

"Buncha liberals in Washington trying to save the planet or some shit."

"Heard that, too."

Francis slapped the notion away. "Hogwash, all of it. These animals are just part of the food chain, see? A natural order of things. Things die—such is the way of nature. How those things die off is of no concern to the laws of the universe."

"Some prominent folks in New York City have a different theory on that, it would seem."

"Well fuck them with a rusty metal pole, because I don't believe a dick's worth," Burner spat. "If they come out and see what we've seen, they'd be spittin' a different tune."

"And what have you found, Francis? Huh? Can you at least tell me that much? If I'm to die, might as well know what it is I died for."

Burner's face sparkled with delight. "What we found...is a journey. To other worlds, my friend." A low and hearty chuckle. "To other worlds."

TANNER FINISHED CUTTING through a *Pteranodon's* face, dissecting the beak from the cranium. One of his men placed gloved hands on the beak and pulled, completely separating the coveted part. Tanner watched the flying reptile's lifeless eyes as the ivory extension came loose, as if he expected them to jump back to life and protest this gross experiment. But they didn't. It was dead, along with several of its brethren.

Today's kills were lined up near the ridge. The survivors that saved themselves from certain butchery were sailing the faded lilac skies, screeching and squawking in mourning for those who had not been so lucky. Tanner glanced up at them, wondering if they could poach one or two more before they lost the day to the encroaching dark. But the row of twelve was enough, certainly beat the afternoon's quota, and Burner would be quite satisfied with the results. Besides, there was always tomorrow. And the next day. And then, after that, they'd have to move on. With Charlie Archer, Nellie Watts, and Finn Hampton showing up—well, there was bound to be more hunters on their trail, and they didn't need that coming to haunt them. No, sir. So, it was time to pack up and move on, get south before winter settled into the bones of Wyoming. Besides, the kills they'd managed were enough to get them through the winter months; that was if Burner's calculations were accurate, which his measurements of such things typically were.

"Drain it there," Tanner said, motioning to the tin bucket positioned next to the downed lizard. A man was already going to work on the wings, chopping and slicing with a massive machete the length of a horse's tail.

The man who was holding the beak looked down at the broken end, eyes full of vacant wonder. "Do you think...I could just have a taste of it?"

Tanner felt his jaw flex tight. "Buddy ol' pal, you best drain that fucker right here and now, and if I see you so much as dip a finger in that, you'll be looking for your teeth out on the canyon floor."

The man's gaze lifted, finding Tanner's eyes. He nodded, and then went to work, angling the beak so the fluid inside dripped down the channels of the nasal cavities and out into the bucket. It was thick like milk on the cusp of curdling and just as white. After the pour, the man shook the beak to make sure every drop was spent. Once he was positive, he must have suspected Tanner had been watching the whole exchange because his eyes darted right back to him.

Tanner glared at him harder than before, as if he could read the man's mind.

"Will you grow red if I ask to lick the wet end?" the man asked, holding up the beak, showing off the emptiness of the canal, but revealing that there was some that could not count toward the bucket. The edge where the nasal soup drained from was glistening.

But Tanner didn't answer. Instead, he turned from the man

and walked over to his second in command, a man named Roth. Tanner didn't know if that was his first or last name, but he was Roth, always had been and always would be, as long as he was in Tanner's company. He didn't get to know his men too well; it made it easier in times like this.

"See that boy over there," Tanner said, choosing to see him as a boy now, because the man clearly had some growing up to do. Not that he'd get the chance.

Roth, who had just finished draining a beak of his own, acknowledged the man's existence. "Aye, I see him."

"He's an addict. Can't have that."

"Okay..." Roth's tone seemed to inquire about what else the situation called for.

"Cut him loose."

"Cut him loose, or cut him loose-loose?"

"The one where he can't be tied back together again, I reckon."

Roth seemed to consider this, as if maybe there was some alternative. But Tanner knew that Roth knew there were no alternatives to his commands, no questioning whatsoever—what was said would be done, or else Roth's strings would be cut just as quickly.

"I'll see it done."

"Very well," Tanner said, and began to walk away. Before he got more than two steps, a great and terrible sound came from somewhere close. It almost sounded like...

"Raptors?" Roth asked, clearly confused. "Not possible."

"Sounded like a raptor call, sure did," Tanner mused, turning his ear toward the sound. "Shit."

"No, no. Raptors don't travel to *Pteranodon* Canyon. No way—they make good pickins for the sky lizards."

"Well shit, Roth—the wind ain't lying to both our ears. I heard it, you heard it." He glanced around at the operation and saw every man had dropped what they were doing to watch the plain, the red, cratered earth that rolled out before them like the surface of Mars. They watched the cacti as if expecting the pack hunters to emerge from behind them, dewclaws extended and seeking flesh. "Everybody heard it."

"Should we check it out?" Roth asked, his voice shakier than Tanner would have liked from his second in command. The man should have been confident, not scared. But...the *Utahraptor* had a way of striking fear into the hearts of men. And although it only sounded like *one*, a lone member astray from its pack, one was enough to do a little damage to a camp like this. It was like playing gun roulette with their lives—just like one of them would catch a bullet, one of them would catch the claw.

"Aye. Take four men. Investigate, report back. And then let's move back to camp before we lose the sun."

Roth nodded, gathered his four best guns, and then rode out.

"You gonna have to try me again," Charlie said, "because I don't think I heard you all that correctly."

"Did you enjoy your trip?" Burner asked. "Before. Your dream. Was it pleasant?"

Dream? Oh, yes, the dream where he saw Burner in the past, standing on that hill, that very vivid representation of the past. That dream?

"Dream?" His senses crawled back to him, piecing together those frames that had come to him while he was unconscious, those striking details he almost accepted as reality. "The dream..."

"Where'd you go?" Burner asked with a grin. "Where'd the juice take you?"

"Juice?" Charlie felt very confused by all this. The dream or the memory, whatever the appropriate title for those moving pictures was, couldn't have possibly been anything but the real thing, an experience out of place. "What juice?"

"Oh, so, they *didn't* tell you then. The government people, I mean. They didn't tell you what the deal was, why we've been out here poaching our hearts out?"

Charlie felt tense from whatever Burner was about to reveal, as if his ride out had been some giant deception, a trick at his expense. Such was the way with government folk. Never straight shooters, them.

"They told me about some act that the president signed, wildlife protection or some such bull, and how science is claiming that the extinction of a particular species could potentially bring about disastrous circumstances for all mankind."

Burner nodded as if he'd heard this claim before, dismissing the entire theory with bark-like laughter. "Oh, those government folks. Sure know how to spin some yarn. But...I'm afraid it's not as complicated as all that."

"Then what is it?"

"It's because of the beaks, the tasty nectar inside them."

Charlie shook his head, unable to comprehend. "Beak nectar? What in tarnation are you talking about, Francis?"

"It's quite simple really. When you crack one of these *Pteranodon's* beaks wide open, there happens to be a delicious liquid lying about in the nasal cavities of these wondrous creatures. Remarkable, isn't it? Now, who the first person was to discover this is beyond me. Had me a guess, I'd pin it on some Indian feller, but that's just me. Anywho, the stuff turned out to be a wicked hallucinogen, affecting the mind in the most astonishing ways, channeling dreamscapes and visions that our minds could not produce on their own accord. The psychoactive properties of the fluid sharpen everything about our dreams, so much so that it's almost like transporting us into an alternate reality."

"Or a real one," Charlie grumbled.

"What was that?"

"I said, or something real." Charlie nodded, referencing an earlier point in time. "Assuming you'd fed me the stuff while I was sleeping. There, I had a dream that I was six years, seven months younger, on that spot out in that Kansas field where you derailed that Number Five. I finally saw you there, on that hill. That moment we locked eyes, though I didn't think it was a true moment, one I actually witnessed...but it felt so damn real."

"The fluid. It brought you back to that moment." Burner looked to the ceiling as if he expected to find God there, or something close to Him. "I wonder if...if because it has something to do with my close proximity to you. As if the fluid knows."

"Maybe the mind knows, and the fluid is just a helper," Charlie suggested, finding himself becoming caught up in this interesting web of drug talk. It was time to cut himself free from it, though. It was time to concentrate on breaking out of here. "So, the government wants to put a stop to it, I suppose."

Burner looked back down on him. "No. They want the fluid for themselves, no doubt so they can tax the shit out of it and sell it for a considerable profit. The government needs their paws in everything, you know that. You know how it is."

Charlie was in no mood for a philosophical debate on how the United States government should conduct themselves. However, he *was* interested in finding out what Burner had in store for his future. "What am I doing here, Francis? I suppose you aren't keeping me neck-kid here for your own kicks."

"Well, no. Mainly keeping you here because there are two more of you on the way, and the only way to catch a rat is with some cheese. Spoiled cheese don't catch no rats, so here the two of you are, one neck-kid white man, one neck-kid Negro, in a cave full of scorpions and who knows what all else. How far off were your pals?"

"I don't know," Charlie admitted, and that was more-or-less the truth. He could have guessed, trotted out some bullshit answer, but Burner would have sniffed it out the second the lie had left the pen. "We got separated a ways back. Could be a day's ride or several. Tanner butchered the horses, so they'd be coming on foot."

"Unless they strapped themselves to the back of a couple *Triceratops,* I'd say that would put them at least two days behind. Which would be today."

Charlie examined Burner, checking for the lie. "Two days? I've been out that long?"

"You've been out for a while now, yes. Don't worry. You didn't miss much. Tanner and his crew are almost finished with the day's poach, and then we'll set up camp not too far from here, a small town we've established our presence in, and then we'll hit the canyons tomorrow. We're almost done here, not too many birds left to shoot out of the sky, so we'll be moving on down south, probably hit up New Mexico for winter, and I hear there's a healthy supply of—" Burner stopped himself, another low grin taking shape on his face. "Why am I telling you this? You ain't gonna be around to see it."

"You gonna kill me, Burner? You gonna end me, allow me to reunite with my family in some great beyond, then you just go ahead and do it. You hear me, you coward! Just go ahead and bring me death."

Amused, Burner chuckled some to himself. "All in good time, my old friend. All in good time."

THE FIVE MEN rode out to the spot of the call, and then brought their horses to a sudden stop. They had taken them up the ridge, following the spiraling bend around and coming to a collection of crags and rocky formations that were passable, though treacherous. This was where Roth had pinpointed the noise, where it had come from. He was sure of it.

Roth dismounted and raised one fist in the air, asking his crew to hold their positions but be on the ready. He didn't see a single dinosaur, not even an infant. There was no evidence of them whatsoever. No tracks, no nothing. He glanced up at the expiring brightness of the day and saw a handful of *Pteranodons* sailing amongst the clouds, and he didn't like being up on the formation so close to them. Roth surveyed the area and then looked over the ridge, down at the camp near the canyons below. He saw Tanner and the other men cleaning up the rest of their mess, tucking the wings and sectioned meat culled from the fallen reptiles' bones into wagons, ready to haul them off back to their stay. Then he looked back to his four men, seeing that all four of them were ready to react to an ambush.

An ambush, he thought. It was a passing thought, but one

that held some traction. Instead of giving it wheels to move, he pulled in the reins. *An ambush, yes. But not from raptors...from...*

Before his eyes widened with the truth, a shot rang out, a loud crack of one, and he watched one of his men's heads disappear behind a misty crimson cloud. The man was flung sideways off his saddle, hit the dirt and stayed crumpled on the dusty terrain.

Roth called on both guns, removing them from their holsters, and flattened himself against the dirt, something his daddy had taught him when he was just a boy and learning how to win a gunfight. *Make yerself a small target,* the old man used to say, one of his first lessons, the kind that didn't revolve around getting smacked with rawhide. *Make yourself hard to hit.*

So, that was what he did on top of that ridge as more shots cluttered the airwaves, the sounds of cracking skies destroying the otherwise silent afternoon. He watched the four men fire at invisible enemies, shooting from where they thought the attack was coming from. But they were inaccurate attempts because the men were shot up all-too quickly, their chests flowering with fresh red as they tried to remain in their saddles. Their bullets sailed onward into the sky, and where they landed would never be discovered.

Roth felt the need to call for backup, but if he did that, shouted down at Tanner and the rest of the gang, he'd give up his position, and then the no-good ambushers would know exactly where he was. So, he stayed silent for a second, hoping that the son of a bitch responsible for this killing spree would reveal himself, inspect the work he'd gone and done. And his patience, as it turned out, was rewarded.

A woman strolled into view, emerging from behind a rock. She walked right over to where the men had fallen, where the horses had scattered.

A woman. Roth couldn't believe it. Not just any woman,

either. That was Elinor Watts, one of the best gunslingers he'd ever heard about. Just what in heckfire was Elinor Watts doing up here at *Pteranodon* Canyon? He'd heard there were bounty hunters on the way, but not once had Tanner or Burner mentioned ol' Nellie. Nope. Not to him. Had they, he might have had second thoughts about taking on the job.

Just a woman, he heard his daddy say. *Just a woman, that's all. Bleeds like anyone else. You just go ahead and pull the trigger now and see for yerself, boy.*

So, he raised his pistols, pointing them ahead, still keeping his body flat against the sandy terrain. Then he heard a click in his ear.

"Best put that down, partner," he heard a man whisper. His eyes didn't leave Nellie Watts's. He saw that she was smiling, as if this was all part of her plan, the whole thing—the faux raptor call, the ambush, her trotting out so she could distract him—all of it. They'd been made fools of.

By a woman.

Roth thought it was best to scream now, call for backup. It was the last play he had. But the second he gathered his breath and opened his mouth, the loudest sound he'd ever heard boomed in his ear, taking away his hearing and everything else as the world cut to black.

FINN LOOKED ASIDE from the splotch of brains and directed his attention back to Nellie. She was pilfering the men's ammo and whatever weapons she could from their persons. The horses had scattered, took off back down the spiraling incline. "They gonna be coming. At least one more wave until they figure out what happened."

"We can't be here when they do," Nellie said, rising to her feet. She quickly checked the chambers of her revolvers and restocked them. Then she slung a Winchester over her back, one she'd stolen off one of the corpses.

"And why is that?" He shook his head. "Let them come to us, I thought that was whole point of mimicking that raptor call. Throat still burns from it; in case you were wondering. No need to thank me or anything."

"You did a lovely job playing raptor and I thank you for your throat's sacrifice," she said with enough snark that Finn thought it couldn't have been anything but intentional. "But you being a dinosaur expert and all, you should know why we can't stay."

He looked to the dead men, then to the sky. "Oh shit."

"Yeah."

The reptilian buzzards were flying lower and lower, and soon they would land to cull the scraps Nellie and he would leave behind.

"Let's go," Nellie said. "There's a path down the backside of this ridge we can use so they don't see us coming. The second wave will be up here when we attack that camp."

"Right," he said, following her down that path. "You think they're keeping Charlie in that cave over yonder."

"Be my guess."

"Think he's alive?"

"I do."

"All right then," he said as they climbed their way down.

In the distance a wild thunder groaned, and the earth trembled in its wake.

"Go on and git," Tanner said to the group of five men who'd saddled up as soon as the shots rang out. "Before they escape."

"You think they comin'? Now?"

It was one of the new idiots they'd picked up back in Utah that had posed the question, and Tanner felt the urge to slap the nose off his face. "Just be prepared for anything."

"What about the birds?" another one asked. He was a veteran on Tanner's crew, someone who'd been relatively quiet over the last few years. His name was Morris, and Tanner couldn't remember ever speaking more than three words to the man over his tenure.

"Get them loaded, quickly. Morris..." he said, as if testing the man's name, trying to verify the correctness of his memory without flatly asking him if that was indeed what his mama called him.

"Yes?" Morris spit some chew onto the red earth below. "What can I do you for, boss?"

"Morris, I need you to take charge down here. Gather the men, get those birds loaded into the wagon like the devil's behind you with a fiery whip. Got it? Then I want you to arm up and prepare for war."

"War, sir?" Morris shook his head. "Just two men. Well, one man. And one woman. How much damage could they do?"

Tanner grimaced. "Complacency has no merit here. Now git going before I change my mind and put Ruiz in charge."

Morris saluted his boss and went on his way, shouting at the troops and getting them out of their wide-eyed stupors.

Tanner scanned the ridges, looking for movement, or another attack. He knew it was coming, but he didn't know where from. They had the high ground and, therefore, the advantage. If they didn't find them first or get their wagons the hell out of there and back to town, then they'd be sitting ducks, easy target practice for the likes of Finn Hampton and Nellie Watts.

Tanner gripped his pistols and watched the surrounding ridges, waiting for the war to begin. He could smell blood and gun smoke in the air, and before nightfall, he assumed, there would be more of it.

So much more.

"Well hell," Barney croaked once Burner had left the cave to go find out what the hell was happening down at the camp, "looks like I gone and messed things up."

"You sure did," Charlie said. He leaned back against the bamboo sticks and sighed. It was starting to get cold, and he longed for a blanket, anything he could throw over his indecent self to keep warm. "Was it the money they were giving you? Is that it?"

"Money helped," Barney admitted. He was a fragment of the wiry old soul Charlie had encountered at the cabin. It was like someone had beaten the spirit right out of him, and Charlie knew someone had. Because Charlie had been through a similar experience, watching his loved ones perish, knowing nothing could be done to prevent it. "Did it for the freedom mostly. Those men, as long as I paid my mystery tax and gave them a clue when someone was coming along once in a blue moon, told them when they had visitors questioning their whereabouts... well, they left me and Marina the hell alone out there. Never known what it was like to be left alone. All my life, someone was working on me. Someone telling me what to do, how to act, how to conduct my goddamn self. But not out there. Not in my cabin by the lake."

Charlie nodded. His anger abated some. He could almost empathize. Still hated what happened and how it all went down, but if Charlie had put himself in the old man's boots, walked around in the life that he'd lived, then maybe, just maybe he could see how that factored into his decision-making.

"The last thing I wanted to do was betray Nellie. Her father treated me the best another man had ever treated me, white man specifically. I tried to send y'all out of the way, as far out as I possibly could without y'all getting suspicious of the directions. Very least I prayed the dinosaurs got you and not Burner's gang. Least the dinosaurs would end you quick."

"Well..." Charlie shrugged. "Thanks for that, I guess."

"Shouldn't have done none of it is the point. I fucked up; I know that, Charlie Archer. Fucked up good and plenty."

"Aye, you did. But that's in the past now, and if we have any shot of getting out of this thing alive, then we best put our noggins together, find some way out of these here cages."

"Gonna be hard considering the situation."

Charlie felt something below him, a tremulous movement. "You hear that?"

The old man froze. Listened. "No."

Charlie placed his ear to the ground and waited. Thirty seconds later, he heard it. Thunder coming from some great distance, and it was getting closer. "Something's coming."

"What?" asked Barney, crawling over to the near side of the cage.

"Don't know. But whatever it is...it's big."

"Did you hear that?" Nellie asked the second she pulled Finn up the small cliff. Looking over her shoulder, past the rusty moonscape of these canyon lands and toward the dimming horizon, she inspected the scenery, looking for the cause of those low grumbles set upon the earth. "It's close."

Finn nodded. "We best keep on moving then."

She turned away from the potential reveal of the noise conductor and moved toward the outlaw camp. Pointing up toward the craggy rocks and canyon cliffs, she spotted dark openings that could only be a cave system—whether these were natural formations or manmade blast tunnels, she couldn't tell, but if she had to wager on where they were keeping Charlie Archer, that was where she'd throw her money.

"Up that a-way," she said, stopping to take a quick breath. She'd reloaded her guns after they had executed those men, but she checked again anyway, just to be sure. It was a bad habit she'd fallen into, but hey—it was better to be sure than unsure, and she had a lot of doubts about her mind lately. She'd been finding it hard to concentrate since they had left Barney's cabin. Seeing the old gunslinger, her father's best friend, flooded her thoughts with childhood memories. Those times spent in town with her daddy, watching him work, keeping the townspeople safe from marauders and criminals of various degrees. She remembered the one time he'd saved twenty people from a bank robbery, rushing into the hostage situation with nothing on but the generic off-duty clothes he had wrapped around himself earlier that morning, picking off each of the robbers one-by-one until they all had fallen. He'd done a lot of heroic things in his time there, but none as memorable as that. The President of the United States, at the time, had sent him a letter of appreciation after news of his bravery had traveled back east. Those were good times. Good times indeed.

And now the old man needed her. This trip out here was not going as smoothly as she would have liked, and she knew the sidesteps and obstructions, pauses in their arrival, put the old man one step closer to death's edge. At this point he had to be looking over that edge, staring down into the great black abyss that was waiting in the afterlife. She hated to think that. The thought summoned a strong sting to both eyes, but it was the truth, and no matter how fast or hard she had ridden out here, the truth would always be waiting on her return.

"You all right?" Finn asked as if he were gauging her thoughts.

"Yes, sir," she said, without skipping a beat. She didn't want him to think she was distracted, that her involvement in this mission was compromised in any way. But she was. Not only was her old man's death looming over her, but there was the betrayal of his best friend in the whole wide world to consider. She still couldn't believe Barney Reeves had sent them through the heart of Dinosaur Alley, had sent them toward the jaws of almost certain death, and had been working for the team of Billy-Boy Tanner and Francis Burner this whole time. She wondered when he'd gone rogue and aligned himself with such villainy. At what point. Before? When he was working for her father? Was he on the take the entire duration of his law enforcement career? Or was this a new endeavor? She hoped to God it was the latter, and she would ask him these questions if she ever got the chance to meet him face to face again. She would ask him, and then, by God, she would hold him responsible for the damage he'd caused. "Let's get up those cliffs. See those caves?"

"I see them."

"That's where we want to be."

Behind them, back where they'd tricked and massacred those gutsy outlaws, they heard guns popping off, rounds firing in rapid succession of each other. And the screeching of flying reptiles, their harsh shrieks echoing across these blasted lands.

"Let's hurry," she said. "Time is against us."

BACK IN THE CAGE, Charlie applied leverage and strength to the gate, hoping the bamboo would bend outward and break, but, even if he had been fully stocked with a good meal and a full-night's sleep, he still wouldn't have been able to manipulate the hard wood. Its strength was absolute and did not give an inch.

"Gonna tucker yourself out." Barney reduced himself to a ball in the corner of his cell. "Not worth the effort, strength you could use for later."

"Might be no later if we can't arrange our escape." Charlie ceased all effort and scooted back to his position opposite the gate. "This place stinks like the dead, and we're beginning to stink with it."

Just then, two shadows appeared at the mouth of the cave. As they got nearer, Charlie saw it was two of Burner's men come to finish the job. He had hoped Burner had big enough stones to finish the task himself, but a part of him was thankful the ride was over, regardless of who ended it.

He glanced down at his naked legs, the scratches that marked the flesh, and closed his eyes, picturing how good it would feel to hold his wife and kid again, feel the softness of their cheeks against his calloused palms, the warmth of their long embrace. If he concentrated hard enough, he could sense the leftover *Pteranodon* juice taking over, showing him very detailed images of the three of them sitting around the dinner table, eating longhorn steaks and squashed potatoes, laughing about some joke that was all-too appropriate, family and wholesome.

Then he opened his eyes and there they were—two rough-neck riders, each with an oversized revolver in hand, big enough hardware to blow holes the size of fists into them.

"Guess this it then?" Charlie asked the executioners. "Guess this is how it ends, guess you cowards are the ones to do it?"

The men did not show him so much as a smile. Instead, they

raised their guns, one for him, one for Barney Reeves, cocked back the hammer and pulled the—

There was a loud bang and Charlie saw a red ribbon of blood stream from the closer man's head. The scene played itself out in almost a slow-motion sort of way. The bullet's exit took with it a splash of scarlet and some chunky globules that couldn't have been anything else but the roughneck's brains, something Charlie would undoubtedly have himself a chuckle about later because he'd been pretty damn sure the son of a bitch wasn't stocking much between the ears. The man fell to the dirt in a glorious sweep of death. The man next to him, who'd still been standing, aiming his revolver at Barney, spun on his heels to face his attacker. Or, as Charlie noticed as he looked on from the corpse and over to the mouth of the cave, *two* attackers.

"Well hell," Barney managed, still unable to capture the gusto he had back at the cabin a few days prior, even though things had taken a favorable turn.

Charlie watched the second roughneck catch two bullets, one with his chest, the other with his neck. Dark red stars exploded as the silver slugs made impact, and the man danced his last jig before his body realized it was dead. He was eternally napping on the earth in no time flat, and after his body lay still, the blood running from his corpse and soaking into the rusty dirt, the two gunslingers made their way down the short path, stepping into the torchlight that washed over the cave's uneven walls.

"Never thought I'd be so happy to see you folks," Charlie said, unable to keep his grin from spreading.

"Back up," Nellie said. "Cover your ears."

He did as she requested.

She fired two rounds into the gate's secure latch and lock. When the gun smoke cleared, the gate swung open.

He was free again.

THE MOMENT BURNER stepped foot in his periphery was the precise moment the *Giganotosaurus* charged the hill where Tanner's men had gone to investigate, and Tanner knew he was fucked harder than a cheap Deadwood whore.

"What is happening?" Burner snapped. *"What the fuck is happening?"*

"I don't know," Tanner admitted, his eyes not leaving the site of that massive creature cresting the ridge. A closer observation, and he saw an arm dangling from the carnivore's mouth. An arm that had belonged to one of his men. The *Giganotosaurus* cocked back its head and swallowed what it hadn't on the first attempt. "But we need to leave and leave now."

"Thought you said these canyons were safe? That carnivores don't hunt here."

Now, Tanner adjusted his line of vision, his cold-eye stare landing on the man who'd caused him quite a bit of agitation over the past few months. "Said it was rare, and it has been. This is the first meat-eater we've encountered out here in months." He pointed to where the beast had come from. "Those intruders must have brought it with them. It could have been hunting their scent."

This answer, though a fairly logical one, didn't seem to sit right with Francis Burner. He scowled at Tanner and stomped his foot in the dirt, kicking up a burnt-orange cloud. "This is ruining my plans! We have a quota to meet! Winter is coming and we'll be forced to—"

Burner's complaints were silenced by a thunderous roar. Every man in camp turned their heads to the top of the cliff where the dinosaur was tilting its snout toward the colorless skies. Its rows of dagger-like teeth were on full display, and no outlaw looked like they wanted to be anywhere close to them. In fact, a few of the workers—despite their allegiances to Burner's cause and the friendly compensation for their commitments—took off running the other way, abandoning their duties.

"Where are you going?" Burner asked the men as they scattered and sought horses to plant themselves on. "Cowards! All of you! I'll kill you!" He pulled out his guns and began firing at them. He had the accuracy of a drunkard nearing closing time, and his bullets bit into nothing save for the dirt and the surrounding rock formations. Dusty clouds bloomed and disappeared just as quickly. "I'll kill you all!"

Tanner knew Burner's blind rage was an immediate concern; the noise would no doubt lure the monster down from its perch, and, once it was down here, there would be no stopping it. All the firepower in camp wouldn't be enough to bring down the tyrant, but it might be enough to avert it from destroying everything they had worked so hard to accomplish here.

"Quiet, you idiot," Tanner said, and he knew a command of this nature would not sit right with Burner. Men were executed for lesser acts of defiance. "You want to bring that thing down here?"

Burner's head craned with a slowness that bordered on inertia. "Excuse me?"

"You heard me. That shoutin' and shootin' is gonna bring

that thing down here, along with every single *Pteranodon* in a three-mile radius. You want that?"

"You want your tongue removed from your skull, boy?" Burner licked his lips like a cannibal seeking to eat the brains of his enemies. "Because if you talk to me like that one more time, I'll cut the pinkness out myself."

"You don't scare me," Tanner said, turning to him, dropping his hand to the grip of his revolver. "You may scare other men easily, but you don't scare me none."

Burner didn't react; he was smarter than that, something Tanner knew, which was what killed him about the way he'd handled the fleeing men. Francis Burner was as smart as a herder's whip, and he should have known that all that noise was like ringing the dinner bell for the giant carnivore.

Burner finally nodded, holstering his guns. "Gather the men who haven't abandoned us in our hour of need. We got two wars to fight. One against that massive creature, and the other against our prisoners' rescuers, including the son of a bitch who took your eye."

At this, Tanner's one eye shot open with alarm. With excitement.

"Oh yes," Burner said, smiling that proud smile that meant he knew a thing or two most in the world did not. "He's here."

FROM THE TOP of the ridge, Nellie and Finn looked out, across the space between them and the *Giganotosaurus*. The massive carnivore had feasted on the men who'd investigated the ambush, torn them to bit pieces. A scattering of limbs littered the top of the ridge around the dinosaur's feet. The towering beast continued to vocalize its victory by shouting at the heavens, its booming sounds echoing across the canyon lands, filling the ears of every living creature within range.

Finn looked down to see some of Tanner's men skedaddling, hopping on their horses, and kicking their spurs faster than they would after a stick-up. The number of men fleeing the scene surprised him, but then again—not really. Tanner never had surrounded himself with reliable folks, certainly not the kind of sycophants the legendary Francis Burner had obtained prior to that infamous train robbery that claimed the lives of almost all his loyal followers. This was Tanner's thrifty nature coming back to bite him.

Finn got a chuckle from that.

"Ready?" he said to Nellie.

Nellie glanced back over her shoulder, and Finn followed her vision to Charlie and Barney. Both men were finishing up clothing themselves and gathering their effects.

"Y'all ready?" she asked them.

The men checked their inventory, the chambers of their guns, and then nodded.

Nellie nodded to Finn.

"Good," Finn said. "And remember—no matter what happens, Tanner is mine."

No one argued with that.

They descended the mountainside, guns drawn, ready to bathe the canyon lands in the blood of those who had wronged the world and robbed the sky of the beautiful creatures that lived there.

THE FIRST BODY DROPPED, a sizable hole opening up on the man's forehead. His friends trampled him as they rode on by, searching for somewhere that wasn't here, away from the enormous carnivore and the four gunslingers that approached from the west side of camp. Most of them got away clean, but a few trapped some bullets with their backs. Some fell from their horses at full speed and tumbled violently across the canyon's red base. Some blindly fired over their shoulders, hitting nothing of discernible value. Those armed souls escaped the area and galloped off toward a setting sun, refusing to look back and see the chaos behind them. But as they rode on, a curious thing happened; the remaining birds in the sky began to dive on them. The four gunslingers watched as the *Pteranodons* swooped down for easy kills, picking off the men, one-by-one, until the herd of riders was significantly thinned. Through the dust the scuffle kicked up, Charlie could see the beaks of the creatures skewering the outlaws' bodies, punching through their chests and stomachs, the narrowed ends penetrating with ease and depositing sloppy piles of innards and other vital parts on the ground below. The unluckiest of men were taken to the skies where several of the *Pteranodons* converged, pecking at various limbs, shearing away flesh and appendages, raining blood from above.

Charlie found himself guilty of watching this massacre with delight. Then he turned his attention to the men gathering below, Burner and Tanner's men, assembling for their final stand, aiming their rifles and pistols and revolvers, striking an intimidating, and coordinated pose. There was a moment where nothing happened, where the men half-hid and crouched behind various objects, natural rock formations and wagons and loading ramps, and that moment of stillness seemed to last several eternities. Charlie could hear nothing but the sound of his own breath. Even the sky-born screeches had ceased their incessant calls, the enormous dinosaur directly north of camp also agreeing to this pact of utter silence.

Then, he heard Burner shout, "Fire!"

Charlie ducked, the barrage of bullets seeming to have a greater range than he'd given them credit for. He managed to dive behind a wagon that stunk of spoiled meats. Nellie was right behind him, sliding in the dirt on her rear, a billow of sand kicking up behind her. He couldn't see where Finn and Barney had bounced off to, and considering the latter's terrible shape, Charlie wondered if the old gunslinger would have gotten anywhere in that condition. He could see in his mind's eye Barney Reeves taking a few to the chest and dying right there on his feet. It was a terrible thought, but he didn't have much confidence in the man's mobility, nor the sharp senses he undoubtedly had once possessed.

They crouched behind the wagon, waiting for a break in the guns' cacophony. He shot Nellie a look and she nodded back, passing the information between them without skipping a beat. The message was this: *I go my side; you go yours; and when we reveal ourselves, we start shooting and don't stop until we're out of bullets or dead.*

Burner's men gave their guns a rest just long enough for Charlie and Nellie to decide the time to move was now. They left their cover from behind the wagon and came out firing. Charlie saw his first three shots make true impacts, and the three men he'd hit went to the dirt, wounded not dead. Wounded was good enough for now. He wasn't looking for kills, he was looking to pare down the numbers. If he could down a few to make things easier, then that was the goal. The killing would come later if there needed to be killing. In Charlie's experience, a downed man was a man who likely gave up the cause, traded his heinous intentions for the sparing of his life. He hoped that was the case with Tanner and Burner's men, but he couldn't be sure. May it be that these men would give their lives to the cause, were prepared to die for their employers.

He sure hoped not. Men who didn't fear death were dangerous men by all accounts.

He kept the firing going, crouching, keeping low to the ground but still moving forward, pressing on the men. He didn't watch Nellie or see if she was handling her section of outlaws with the ease or accuracy he had—he simply didn't want to take his eyes off his targets, risk missing a single shot. But he listened. Listened to the loud sounds of her guns singing their songs of death, crying out, echoing through the canyon lands, reaching every ear engaged in this bloody battle.

Charlie took out another three men. One he'd shot right in the face, watched his jaw disappear in a bloody detonation of skin and bone. The other men were shot in the shoulders, their entire bodies spinning as they fell to the earth.

Burner screamed for all hands to carry guns and return fire. He screamed and demanded victory.

And something screamed back.

That was when the *Giganotosaurus* stepped foot onto the battlefield, looking to engage in the action and pick up whatever scraps it could.

Finn was firing on a pair of men, pumping their bellies full of silver, when the carnivore's massive foot planted in the earth, squashing one of Tanner's men. Tanner, who wasn't too far from the creature, looked up and screamed in fright. Finn had never seen the man scream, do anything except bark harsh orders and tongue-lash his underlings. But now, the man cowered in fear of the giant beast whose shadow blanketed him.

The *Giganotosaurus* leaned forward, opening its jaws, seeking a fresh kill. One outlaw, a man with a red bandana around his throat, screamed out as he raised his revolvers and fired into the dinosaur's open maw. The bullets did nothing, and the *Giganotosaurus* brought its teeth together, crunching the man's body between them. The impact squished the man, and Finn watched utter shock explode across his features as his innards were reduced to jam inside him. Gouts of blood flew from the sheer violent force the animal had brought to the bite, and then the *Giganotosaur* hoisted him into the air, where it chewed his life from him, reducing the man's body to rags of flesh and dripping crimson.

Finn took the opportunity to put a bullet in Tanner's leg, the shot exploding through Tanner's knee, painting the surface of the formation behind him with the bright scarlet starburst. Tanner went to the ground, clutching the wound in agony, crying out for a God Finn was pretty sure he didn't believe in. Finn had hoped the religious moment would be enough to attract the attention of the carnivore, but it was the gunshot that swept his eye. Finn stared at the *Giganotosaurus,* and, for a moment, they were locked in a children's staring contest. It was like the creature wasn't so sure it wanted to pursue this man, as if the man was dangerous, as if those two boom cannons in both hands would cause it harm. The only thing that passed through Finn's mind was how fast he would die if the *Giganotosaurus* charged. And then the dream came to him, the nightmare back in Oat Creek, the one he sometimes got about dinosaurs eating him—because, after all, it had been dinosaurs that had killed his parents and made him an orphan when he was nine years old, and he suddenly realized that he was here because of dinosaurs, that dinosaurs had influenced every decision in his life ever since that harrowing moment, ever since those two *Tyrannosaurs* gobbled up mommy and daddy. Dinosaurs had ruined him but also made him, and maybe that was why he found them so fascinating. Like, even now, as he looked up at the towering monster, he felt a closeness to it, like he was a part of its life. Maybe that was the drugs he'd been taking, the left-over dream smoke affecting his brain, his thoughts, but he thought in some way it was true; all living creatures were somehow related, connected by some current that lives through all things, born from the chasm that existed somewhere beyond the stars. Stardust, that was all they all were. Floating in the cosmos, drifting toward the outermost reaches of space and time.

The psychedelic afterthoughts were confusing, and Finn did his best to forget them. The towering monster lunged forward with a surprising quickness. Finn cursed, fired two shots that hit the target—the *Giganotosaurus's* chest—and then sped off in the opposite direction, seeking the first thing that qualified as shelter. That shelter came in the form of a shallow cave that had been cut into the base of the canyon. He sprinted toward it and slid on his backside, and when the cover was over him, he spun around to look back out, drawing his aim and keeping that aim true.

The enormous head of the *Giganotosaurus* closed out all remaining light, drenching Finn and the shallow cave in absolute darkness. Finn smelled the odoriferous breath being puffed out of the nostrils atop its snout. It was like the wind carrying the stink of fallen soldiers after a bloody, brutal battle, a stench that could travel miles and miles across the lands marked by death. Finn shot several rounds into the snout, and the loud bangs, with nowhere to travel, knocked out his hearing, the sounds of eager grunts of hunger now replaced by a low, perpetual ring. The bullets had torn gaping holes in the creature's tough flesh, and it seemed like the damage was enough to make it retreat, at least for the moment. As the massive carnivore's head jerked away and out of sight, light beamed back in. Finn inched himself to the end of the cave and glanced up at the light, expecting to see the monster hovering over the opening, waiting for Finn to expose himself to the late afternoon. But he didn't see the monster's teeth waiting for him. Instead, he saw the *Giganotosaurus* lumbering away from the scene, searching for other potential victims to subject its teeth to.

Finn took a breath and slid out.

A bullet tore off from somewhere close, punching into his shoulder, knocking him down against the red earth. He would stay there until a shadow fell over him, a shadow that was synonymous with death.

That shadow belonged to Billy-Boy Tanner; he was limping, bleeding, and the smile he flashed was filled with broken teeth. "I see you," Tanner said, and Finn knew he was about to die.

CHARLIE WATCHED with mean eyes as Burner clambered into the back of a wagon, the outlaw bastard's face fixed with a heinous snarl. With force, he kicked off a few dead *Pteranodons*, making room for himself and a few of his men. One of the outlaws climbed behind the horses and grabbed a whip, shouted, "Hee-yaw!" before cracking the two tan beauties on their necks. With that, the wagon was off, launching across the canyon like a rock from a slingshot.

Charlie refused to let the man get away this time. He took some Hail-Mary shots at the wagon, a few pops that died in the distance, and Nellie joined in to do the same, shooting both guns, but she missed hers as well, and the wagon was getting farther and farther out of reach.

"Shit," Charlie cursed, and then sprinted over to the first wagon he could find, the *only* one he could find. Luckily the two mares who were attached had not freaked out about the chaos behind them and had stayed rooted to the canyon floor. Charlie climbed into the wagon and then turned to Nellie and Barney. "Old man, you steer us straight on. Follow that wagon into Hell if you have to."

"Well hell, I suppose I could." Barney hustled over to the horses as fast as he could, which wasn't very fast at all.

"What about Finn?" Nellie asked, taking Charlie's hand and hopping into the wagon.

"What about him?"

"He could be..." She scanned the distance between them and the enormous dinosaur that had torn through what remained of Burner's camp. Tents and people lay scattered around it, a mess of fabric and blood and body parts. Charlie did not envy the team that had to clean up this mess, reassemble the bodies and ship them back to their families (if they had any) so they could receive proper burials. Charlie didn't think any of Burner's men deserved such traditions, and, if the law was looking for volunteers to help the cause, he'd leave himself out of it.

"What?" Charlie asked. "Dead?"

Nellie nodded as Barney cracked the whips and got the horses moving.

"He could be," Charlie said. "He very well could be, but that's not our concern, not right now. Our concern..." He pointed up ahead, where Burner's getaway wagon kicked up storms of dust, making it almost impossible to see the trajectory of his path. "...our concern is Burner and nothing else."

The wagon took off, and the chase was on.

FINN WAS BLEEDING PRETTY good when Tanner got his revolver up, pointing it at his face. He laid himself down on the hard surface of the rock beneath him, resting his head so he could look up at the sky's expanse one last time before he died. Breathing in so deep that the air touched his soul, he smiled.

"Your death funny to you, cowboy?" Tanner asked, and Finn heard the click of the gun readying itself to end him. "You always were a peculiar asshole."

"It's just...that none of this matters."

"Fuck you talking about?"

"Life. So insignificant, you know?"

"You took my eye, motherfucker. You took my goddamn eye from me!" Tanner reached down and grabbed Finn's throat. He picked him up and slammed him into the rocks. Finn's head bounced hard off the surface, and dark stars flooded his vision. "Don't tell me that none of this matters! Have you ever tried to live with one eye? Have you?! It's awful. The way people look at you, the way *women* look at you! Like you're some kind of filth! Some kinda lesser man!"

"See," Finn said, gurgling with laughter, "and I always thought it made you look so much prettier."

The fist came in a flash and Finn had no time to react. Tanner's knuckles connected with his chin, and Finn's head snapped to the side, and he fell back down.

"You horse's testicle, I ought to shoot you right here and now," Tanner said.

Finn felt cold metal on his neck. "Then do it. What are you waiting for?"

"No." The cold pressure was released. "No, you don't deserve a quick way out. I'm going to beat you to death, like you earned it."

Finn didn't feel much like getting up to get punched some more.

"Get up, you son of a bitch. Fight me like a man."

Slowly, he got to his feet while checking his chin to make sure it hadn't been knocked off. "You pack a good punch there, Tanner."

"Well, there's more where that came from, cowboy."

Tanner lunged forth and threw a haymaker, but Finn was able to sidestep this one. He let Tanner's momentum carry him toward the formation, and, when Tanner's hands were pressed against the craggy surface, Finn delivered an uppercut to the man's ribs. Tanner winced in pain, but he quickly recovered, spinning and facing his attacker with hands out, his southpaw stance not particularly threatening.

"Gonna smash yer face to bits," Tanner promised.

Finn only smiled.

The two men fought on, throwing fist after fist at each other, each landing a considerable number of shots, but neither able to procure the knockout shot they were hoping for. Finn bloodied his knuckles on Tanner's face, and Finn's face was full of running red as well. It looked as if the two men could drag this out forever, neither able to gain advantage over the other.

Finn checked the status of the *Giganotosaurus* and saw the creature was hanging back a safe distance away, sticking its snout in the guts of a fallen gunslinger, lapping up the blood with its tongue. In the three seconds he had taken his eyes off Tanner, Tanner reacted by digging out a sharp arrowhead he'd kept in his pocket and had come at Finn with a swiftness that would match a *Utahraptor's*. But Finn was faster, and he was able to catch the arrowhead with his forearm before Tanner could run it across his throat. The stubby blade bit into his flesh, sinking through the muscle and hitting his bone. The pain was incredible and pounded through him like a *Triceratops* in a taproom. After about five seconds of watching Tanner drag the arrowhead down his forearm, splitting open the flesh and sepa-rating the muscle beneath, he withdrew his arm and kicked Tanner square in the love pouch between his legs. It wasn't the manliest tactic, but the situation had called for it, and, well, Tanner definitely more than deserved it. The bastard named Billy-Boy Tanner tried to ignore the jolt of pain pulsing through his privates, or at least pretended like it hadn't affected him, but as the moment wore on, the pain became increasingly evident, and Tanner walked bowlegged toward him, like a drunk stumbling to bed.

"You...coward," Tanner said, spittle flying from his lips. His voice had changed then; not higher like a eunuch's, not like Finn had expected, but a low, growly voice, like a father telling his kid a spooky campfire tale and imitating the monster in the story. "You...fucking...coward."

Tanner slashed the air before him, seeking Finn's throat. Finn backpedaled, able to keep his balance on the uneven surface of the rocky terrain.

Then, booming. Loud. Getting closer.

The earth shook with a hellacious sound, a roar that caused Finn's hearing to shut off. A drowning, warbling noise entered his ear canals.

Finn turned just in time to see an open mouth like a cave, ivory stalactites and stalagmites that would have no problem tearing him apart in less time than he could blink. Finn didn't think about his next move; he just reacted. His instinct was to drop to the ground, flop there and play dead, which wasn't the best plan considering he'd just seen the animal eating from the motionless dead a few minutes ago. But that was what he did, and when he dropped, he was surprised the *Giganotosaurus* bypassed him. He was easy prey, but the carnivore had something else in mind.

"NO!" Tanner shouted, and it was the last thing he'd ever utter. The huge mouth of the dinosaur bit down on him, covering everything from his hips on up. There was a wet crunch and a rubbery squeak, and then the gigantic creature rose up, the limp legs of Billy-Boy Tanner dangling from its mouth.

As the *Giganotosaurus* kicked its head back and devoured its kill, Finn scrambled to his feet and sped back over to the small inlet where he'd hidden himself earlier. Once there, he crawled inside and examined his wounds, doing everything he could to stop the bleeding. But sooner or later, it was all too much.

He became drowsy. And when the darkness came, he didn't fight it.

SPEEDING THROUGH THE CANYON LANDS, the wagon had caught up to the one in front of it. Charlie, standing up on the driver's bench, leaned forward and aimed through the clouds of chalky earth particles. He fired shots at the shadowy outline of Burner's ride but couldn't confirm whether or not they landed. The mystery of his efforts was not good enough, and as good as a shot he thought he was, he was fairly certain the bumpy conditions had caused him to miss. He recalculated and shot some more, until his chambers ran empty.

"Damn it," he muttered, and Nellie must have heard him, because she came up beside him and offered him a handful to reload with. "We ain't getting close enough," he told her. And then he barked at Barney, "Can you scoot alongside them?"

"Well hell! I'm trying!"

The old cowboy whipped those horses, kicking them into a gear higher than Charlie suspected they had. The gap between both parties closed some, and within a quarter click, they were close enough Charlie thought he could jump and land on Burner's back.

Through the dirty haze, he saw Burner glancing back, those soulless eyes beaming like a Jack-O-Lantern's. There was Hell in those eyes, for sure, and Charlie Archer thought it was about time to send the man to the underworld where he belonged.

A flash appeared in the haze, and Charlie felt something punch through his chest. The impact knocked him on his rear, and when his eyes looked down to where the pain had blossomed, he saw a splash of red dripping through a nice hole above his heart.

"Shit," he muttered, and tasted copper on his tongue.

"Charlie!" Nellie cried out as she helped the man down, so he didn't fall and fall alone. "Charlie!"

He was confused some, the scene not quite adding up. Had he been shot? By Burner? It didn't make sense, and it sure as hellfire wasn't supposed to end this way. Not with him getting shot and Burner making it away.

You were supposed to kill him, daddy, he could hear his boy saying. *Supposed to kill him for ma and me.*

But, with the considerable amount of red leaking out of him and the pain that was funneling through his arms and legs, his body all over, he didn't think that was still in the cards.

"You're shot," Nellie said.

He coughed, and blood danced over his bottom lip, spilling down his chin. "Will I live?" It was the first question that came to mind. He didn't care one way or the other, but if he was to die, then he'd like to know it.

"I...I don't know."

"Burner?"

Nellie glanced up, ahead. "He's dead. You got him."

"Really?" Blood filled his mouth, and all he could taste was pennies. The pain was insurmountable now, had seeped into every nerve. "Dead?"

"Deader than dead. You shot him good, Charlie Archer."

"Well..." he said, sniffing out something funny in the way she spoke through the sadness. He couldn't tell if she was kidding him or not, but in what was probably going to be his final moments, there was no sense in arguing with her. "Am I going home, Nellie Watts?"

With tears in her eyes, she nodded. "Yeah, I think so."

He blinked and then he could see them—his wife and kid, standing in an open meadow, sunlight raining down on them in magnificent cones, a sparkling lake to their left, and the magenta mountains at their backs. Both smiling, both happy, because he was there with them now. And in that place there was no pain, nothing but the heavenly touch of this happy dreamworld.

He blinked again, and a great darkness swallowed him up, stealing him forever.

NELLIE WATCHED life fade from Charlie Archer's eyes, and then she took about three seconds to mourn the crushing loss, and then the time to mourn was over. The time to kill had just begun. She checked her two best friends to make sure they were fully loaded, and they were. Facing her adversaries, the wagon that had expanded the gap between them, she steadied her aim and squinted through the dust storm.

"Keep driving straight, old man," Nellie said to Barney.

"Well hell, not sure the horses can hold up much longer!" he shouted over the galloping and bouncing of the wooden wheels against the canyon's rough terrain.

"You keep it straight and true until those horses are dead, or you are," she said, and then raised her revolvers at the dusky outline of the enemy's ride.

She fired, concentrating on those vague shadows she thought were men, evil men, men that deserved to die out here where no one would find them save for the buzzards of this thirsty, dry earth. She continued to squeeze the triggers until there was nothing left to throw at them, and then reached for the reload. The distance between the carts was still too great, and she couldn't confirm whether the shots were landing or not. She hadn't seen anyone slump over the side, so she suspected her aim had missed.

After reloading, she bent toward Barney's ear. "Closer, old man. Get us closer and now."

He growled like something feral, and then whipped the horses with a fury she'd never seen him unleash before. She couldn't tell if their horses quickened in that moment, or the ones in front of them slowed down, but the gap narrowed, and Nellie could see Burner's face through the tan haze that encompassed these canyon lands. That demented smile, that devilish laughter that rang out over the horses' clopping and the wagon wheels' turning. She aimed and put a bullet right where it belonged.

Burner's smile died immediately as he looked down to see cherry leaking from a new thumbhole on the chest of his jacket. The spill ran out of him like the pour hole in a wine barrel, and he clutched the wound immediately. Trying to raise his gun to return the favor, the man struggled. He only managed to get his arm halfway to the position needed before his fingers failed him, and the gun fell to the wagon's deck. Two men came over to check on their boss, and Nellie pounded them with new shots, three for each, and she watched with delight as the men went over the side of the wagon and tumbled along the dusty trail behind them in violent revolutions.

When she returned her eyes to the enemy's wagon, there was another man in position on the rear, two guns out and fingers already applying pressure to the triggers. She didn't have time to meet him, so she ducked, and yelled out for Barney to—

It was too late. The gunfire exploded through the canyons, and she watched four holes blossom on Barney Reeves's back, each flowering with petals of wet crimson. One last shot tore through the right side of his face, and, when Nellie glanced up, she saw his cheek and most of his neck had peeled away, revealing a dark cavern of blood and scrunched muscle that the bullet had displaced on its passing through. Then the man crumbled over and fell into the wagon atop her.

She quickly flipped him over and stared at his dead eyes; there were no last words here, no chance to tell him that she forgave him for his mistakes, that he was still the best second father she never asked for. She couldn't get the words out. It was too late and there was no time to waste; there was one more kill to make before the deed was done.

Nellie stood up and faced the proud gunslinger, who was now caught reloading his revolver. She raised her gun and with little effort, put a bullet through his eye. The gun clapped and the man's brains slipped out where the silver nugget made its grand exit, and then the body went limp as it careened over the edge of the wagon, disappearing into the dusty clouds below.

The horses kept moving, but with no drivers they slowed. Nellie made her way to the front where Barney had held his position through the gunfight, and then she saw that the wagon before her was empty save for the lone driver. The man with the scruffy white beard and a drunkard's red complexion glanced over his shoulder back at Nellie, and Nellie nodded to him, letting him know it was time to get off at the first available opportunity or...die. The man didn't hesitate; he dropped the reins, tucked, and rolled off the side, disappearing along with his fallen comrades. If he lived, he lived. Nellie was done killing for the day, or so she hoped. She had one thing to check before leaving *Pteranodon* Canyon behind, forever.

She directed the horses ahead, driving the wagon parallel with Burner's crew, and then headed off the opposing horses. She was able to get them to slow, and, about thirty gallops later, she forced them toward the canyon walls, making them stop completely. She boarded the other wagon, gun drawn in case her shots were not as effective at killing as she had previously thought, and then proceeded to inspect the dead, carefully. Burner's men were goners, not a single breath emanating from their still bodies. But Burner...

Burner had managed to live.

His breaths were shallow, but present and wheezy. His eyes were rolling, and Nellie could tell he was doing everything he could to stay conscious, to walk away from the white light at the end of that eternally dark canyon. She knelt next to him, keeping her gun in a position that would deliver him an instant death should this be a ruse of sorts. Once she was beside him, she could tell there was no trick in Burner's cards—only death's impending cuddle.

His eyes migrated to hers. She nodded, then took his hand away from the wound so the opening could leak faster. There was no resistance; it was like moving a thin branch out of her way. The red trickled out of the bullet hole, splashing down his clothing, soaking into the fabric. Soon, the steady flow began to pool, having lost its thin nature and gained its clot.

"You're dying, Francis Burner," she told him, just in case he was mistaken about the situation. "And I'm going to sit here and watch you die, so there ain't no confusing it this time. And then..." She looked to the sky, saw a whole flock of *Pteranodons* patrolling the nebulous glow above. "...then I'm gonna haul you to Washington and throw your corpse on the President's porch. And that's just what I'm gonna do."

He opened his mouth to speak, and, instinctively, as if she'd given the action absolutely no thought, she shot him in the face, and didn't even flinch when the back of the man's head blew off and caked the back of the wagon, coating the old wooden slats in soupy strokes of brains and blood.

She leaned back against the wagon's boards and sighed. The ride was over. She would gather Burner's body in the back of the other wagon, along with Charlie's and Barney's.

The rest of the fallen she would leave for the birds.

GRAVES

Charlie Archer's burial went off without a hitch, and there were only six people in attendance. Nellie Watts, Finn Hampton, some preacher whose name was never disclosed, two undertakers, and Oliver "Smitty" Smith, who'd come all the way out from Washington. The latter was probably in the area on other business, but he'd been gracious enough to stop by and offer his condolences.

Finn shook the man's hand, using his left because his right was done up in a sling on account of where Tanner had shot him. "Thanks for dropping by," he said, though Nellie thought he hardly meant it. Maybe he did. Despite his crooked past, Finn had turned out to be quite the surprise. "Charlie would have appreciated you coming and visiting and all."

"It's the least I could do for his service," Smitty said, turning and signaling the Stations of the Cross as the undertakers began to shovel dirt over the coffin. "At least he's with his wife and kid now, God bless them all."

Nellie glanced at the two gravestones next to where Charlie was going. She was glad they were together again too, though she didn't have much belief in the mysticism of the Christian Catholic afterlife. She didn't know what she believed in these days but figured that was what she could use the remainder of her life for—more philosophy and less killing.

"And Miss Watts," Smitty said, turning to her. The politician extended his hand and offered a slight bend of his knee. "I am absolutely destroyed to hear about the untimely passing of your father."

"He was very sick," she told him, taking his fingers, giving them a slight squeeze. "But he's in a better place now, I reckon."

"You reckon correctly, m'dear. You reckon correctly."

He pulled his hand back and flashed them a gaping smile. "Well, I really must be off. There's a ton of work to do, but I can't thank the two of you enough for coming through for our country. The President sends his warmest regards."

"I bet he does," Nellie said, nodding.

"If you all are ever in the need of work, just send the word and I'll be happy to supply you with work that pays quite handsomely."

"I'll give it careful consideration."

Finn motioned to his bad arm. "Guess when I'm repaired, I'll be in touch. Ain't got nothing planned and a little honest, legal work is something I could get used to."

Smitty smirked. "Honest. Yes. Well, I look forward to that, Mr. Hampton. I thank you for your kindness and your company the day after those brutish creatures came to Oat Creek."

"My pleasure."

Smitty tipped his hat, and then he headed for the horse and wagon that was waiting for him near the end of the graveyard.

Once he was gone, Nellie turned to Finn. "Thought you were off to write a book about the beautiful creatures of this world?"

Finn nodded like he knew he'd been caught in a small lie.

"Maybe that's for other folks to figure out and not Finn Hampton."

"Who is Finn Hampton?"

He shrugged. "Guess that's for other folks to figure out, too." A warm smile touched his face, but she wasn't comforted by it. "Who do you think Finn Hampton is?"

"I think Finn Hampton is a man with good intentions, who sometimes makes some dumb decisions."

"Can't argue with that."

"Goodbye, Finn."

She turned, and he caught up to her in a few long steps.

"Now wait a minute," he said, jogging in front of her, turning so she couldn't continue on her path forward. "What about us?"

"Us?"

"You and me."

"There is no you and me, you jackass."

She tried to step around him, but he blocked her.

"Well...why the heck not?"

"You know why, Finn."

"Do I?"

"You should, unless you are as dumb as you look."

"Now, look, I'm a good man. You just done said so yourself."

"No, I said you're a man with good intentions. Not the same as a good man."

This bit of news seemed to stump him, and when she motioned to move around him, this time he didn't stop her.

She walked about twenty paces toward the falling sun, that orange blaze that had set fire to the horizon, and then stopped to face him one last time. "I hope you find yourself, Finn Hampton. And I hope you like what you locate."

With that she turned. Walked. Toward the sun where a herd of Sauropods lumbered, their heavy footfalls sounding off like distant thunderclap.

"Well, where you going?" Finn asked.

But she didn't answer him. Mostly because she didn't know the answer herself.

The world was vast, and so were the possibilities.

ABOUT THE AUTHOR

Tim Meyer dwells in a dark cave near the Jersey Shore. He's written and published over fifteen novels and novellas, including *Malignant Summer*, *The Switch House*, *Dead Daughters*, *Limbs*, and many other titles. His screenplay adaptation for *The Switch House* has won two finalist awards (Semifinalist, Screen-Craft Horror Competition 2020 & Semifinalist, Filmmatic Horror Screenplay Awards 5). He exists on coffee and IPAs.

You can visit him at timmeyerwrites.com.